The Great
SCIENCE FAIR
Disaster

**Other Apple Paperbacks
you might enjoy:**

I Spent My Summer Vacation Kidnapped Into Space
by Martyn Godfrey

The Mall from Outer Space
by Todd Strasser

The Secret Life of Dilly McBean
by Dorothy Haas

Shoebag
by Mary James

Sixth Grade Secrets
by Louis Sacher

Tales from Academy Street
by Martha Derman

The Great SCIENCE FAIR Disaster

Martyn Godfrey

AN
APPLE
PAPERBACK

SCHOLASTIC INC.
New York Toronto London Auckland Sydney

For my good friend, Kristy Staples.
Thanks for the inspiration.

ISBN 0-590-44081-0

12 11 10 9 8 7 6 5 4 3 2   2 3 4 5 6 7/9

Printed in the U.S.A.   28

First Scholastic printing, November 1992

1.
The Great Idea

My father walked into my seventh-grade classroom, looked around, and smiled. Oh, no, I thought. He's going to do it again.

"May I interrupt the lesson to speak to your students, Ms. Rand?"

"Of course," Ms. Rand, my homeroom and science teacher, answered.

Dad continued to smile as he walked to the front of the class. That wasn't a good sign.

My best friend, Alison McBride, who sits next to me, leaned over and whispered, "What's up, Marcie?"

"I don't know," I whispered back.

My father, Mr. Grigg Wilder, is the principal of the Fifth Street School in White Falls, Montana. I'm a student in the same school.

Dad pulled a handkerchief from his pocket and wiped it across his bald head. He always sweats on top when he's excited or nervous.

"How are we today, boys and girls?" he asked.

Most of the class said "Fine." A few people said "Good." I heard Steve Butz say "Rotten." My father didn't hear him. When everyone speaks at once, it sounds like "Murmurkle."

"That's good." Dad smiled. "Are you enjoying our cold November weather today?"

My "of course not" was buried under the "Murmurkle."

"I have a great idea," he went on.

I was right. Dad was doing it again. Another Great Idea.

"Would you like to hear it?"

"Murmurkle."

"Good, good," he said. "I think it would be wonderful for the seventh graders to hold the First Annual Fifth Street School Science Fair. Do you know what a science fair is?"

"Murmurkle."

"Well, Ms. Rand will give you the details later. But for now, what you need to know is that each of you will have to make a science project. Everyone will make something that we can display in the gym a week from Friday. You may work alone or with a partner. You are going to create something that shows science at work."

"Ewww, that sounds like fun!" Jennifer Jensen squealed.

"Ewww," Steve mimicked.

"That's enough of that," Ms. Rand warned Steve. "You will treat your classmates with proper deference. Do you understand?"

"Yes, Ms. Rand," Steve mumbled, even though I bet he doesn't have a clue what *deference* means. Even I had to look it up.

"The science fair will be a contest, as well," my dad went on. "The best project will win a fifty-dollar prize."

A symphony of *ohs* and *ahs* greeted that announcement.

"I will be a judge," Dad concluded. "And Mrs. Bompas, the head of our school board, will also be a judge. Doesn't that sound terrific?"

"Murmurkle. Murmurkle."

I'm not so sure, Dad, I thought. I always get nervous when I hear another one of your great ideas. ·

"I'm not so sure," I told Alison as we changed clothes for gym. "I always get nervous when I hear another one of his great ideas."

"I think it'll be okay," she said. "We'll have a good time making a project together."

After I pulled on my T-shirt, I went to the mirror to tie my hair into a ponytail. Alison stood beside me to do the same thing.

"I think I've grown a little. I'm taller than you are," she said.

"No, you're not. Your sneakers have thicker soles. That's all."

Alison and I are the same height and we both

have long hair. But that's where our similarities end. She has blonde, wavy hair. Mine is brown and *very* straight. She has sea-blue eyes. Mine are brown. She's got a shape already. I don't.

"You know how some of my father's great ideas don't work out," I said. "Maybe this science fair will be one of them."

"What can go wrong?" she asked.

"That's what my father said about pet day in fifth grade. Remember that?"

"Of course I do." Alison chuckled.

What a day *that* had been. Dad had decided it would help raise school spirit if everyone brought their pets to class for a day.

"I'm not sure, Dad," I'd said. "Maybe it's not a good idea to have all those animals in school at the same time. I mean, don't some pets eat other pets?"

"Don't worry about it, Marcie," Dad had told me. "I've made a rule that each pet has to be in a cage or on a leash. What can go wrong?"

Lots of stuff.

My father should have known what would happen when seven dogs, five cats, three hamsters, two mice, two budgies, one goldfish, one boa constrictor, and one ferret met for the first time in the same classroom.

It's not easy holding a Saint Bernard on a leash when it smells odor-of-cat. It's even tougher hold-

4

ing a cat on a leash when it sees a Saint Bernard charging at it. A rampaging Saint Bernard and a screeching cat can sure do the job on a budgie cage when they bowl into it. And it's best not to talk about the boa and two of the hamsters.

"Some pet day," I said to Alison. "And I've got a feeling that the First Annual Fifth Street School Science Fair could end up the same way."

Lunch was after gym. Alison had choir practice, so I went to the cafeteria by myself. I stood in line for the hot meal.

My mother, Sharon the fitness freak, always makes me buy hot food at noon. She figures it's more nutritious than a sandwich and a Twinkie.

I'm sure she'd change her mind if she had to eat a Fifth Street School hot lunch.

My father hired a new cook last month. Her name is Mrs. Rene Bawlf. She looks like the wicked witch in *The Wizard of Oz* and she's terrible at her job.

She makes the weirdest things. Her favorite is something she calls Organ-Meat Helper. We have it once a week.

Steve butted in front of me. "You don't mind if I butt in, do you?"

"Yeah, I do," I snarled.

"Well, too bad," he snarled back. " 'Cause I just did. What are you going to do about it? Tell your

5

old man?" Then he started talking in a baby voice: "Daddy, Daddy, big, bad Stevie butted in front of cute, little old me."

My first reaction was to break my tray over his fat head. But you can't do stuff like that when you're the principal's daughter.

"Hey, Marcie, wipe the angry look from your face," Steve said as we shuffled down the line. "It makes you look uglier."

"You're a jerk!"

"Oh!" He held his hand over his mouth as if he were surprised. "I'm a *jerk*. Thanks for telling me. All this time I thought I was a nice guy."

We moved closer to Mrs. Bawlf.

"I'm sorry, Marcie." He grinned at my sour face. "I got to be me."

"Why don't you try being somebody else for a change? Somebody human."

"Good one," he said. "There's hope for you yet."

"More than I can say for you."

"On a roll," he chuckled. "Your little brain must be working overtime."

Maybe my dad *would* understand if I took a swing at Steve.

We moved to the serving counter.

"Good day, Mrs. Bawlf," Steve said.

"Sure, sure," she mumbled as she handed him his lunch.

"See you, Helium Brain," Steve said to me as he headed for one of the seventh-grade tables.

6

I growled at him.

Mrs. Bawlf passed a plate to me, and I examined the food. My lunch was six little black things that looked like fried mud.

"Excuse me, Mrs. Bawlf," I asked. "What are we eating today?"

"Liver nuggets," she told me.

"Liver nuggets?" I whispered to myself. "Liver nuggets?"

"Oh, I forgot." Mrs. Bawlf placed a small paper cup on my tray. It was full of thick, green glop.

"What's this?" I asked.

"The dipping sauce," she told me. "Sweet-and-sour broccoli paste."

I studied the contents of my tray for several seconds.

"Move on," Mrs. Bawlf ordered. "There are other people in line."

"Can I ask you a question first?"

She dropped her head and looked at me under her bushy, gray eyebrows. Maybe she thought I was about to say something rude.

And for a moment, that's exactly what I was planning to do. I was going to say, "Why would anyone, anywhere, want to eat a liver nugget? If I hadn't eaten in three weeks, I wouldn't want a liver nugget! How could you even think of a liver nugget?"

But I didn't. It was the principal's daughter thing again. I knew I'd never be able to explain that to my father as "Just a slip of the tongue, Dad. I didn't even know I said it."

So in my politest voice, I asked, "Are we ever going to have hamburgers and French fries?"

"On Friday, we're having quahog-burgers," Mrs. Bawlf told me.

"Quahog-burgers? What's a quahog?"

"It's like a clam, only bigger," she said.

"We're going to have clam-burgers for lunch?"

She shook her head. "No. We're having quahog-burgers."

That did it. "Quahog-burgers? Mmmm. How wonderful!" I said sarcastically. "I can't wait. A taste treat. They sound delicious."

"Don't talk to me in that tone of voice," she huffed. "I'm going to tell your father."

2.
Vitamin A
and Poetry

I walked over to a table and joined three of my classmates. Jennifer Jensen, Winfred Falkingham, and Tony Alfredo were already eating their lunch.

I sat down and watched Winfred nibble on a piece of green-dipped, brown stuff. He was obviously enjoying his meal.

"You like those, Winny?" I asked.

He looked at me through his thick glasses. "Oh, yes," he answered. "Liver is a good source of vitamin A. The latest findings say that vitamin A is needed for the smooth running of our immune system."

"No kidding?" I said as I scraped the six lumps from my plate onto Winfred's. "This is for your immune system."

"Thanks," Winfred smiled. "You really are nice."

"I'm trying to cut back on the liver," I told him. "I had liver flakes for breakfast."

He made a serious face, then broke into a smile. "That's a joke, right?"

I nodded.

He laughed.

I turned to Tony. "How about you?" I asked. "You like today's lunch?"

"I'll eat anything," Tony answered. "Anything at all. I don't care what it tastes like. As long as it's food, I'll eat it."

Maybe Jennifer felt the same way about Mrs. Bawlf's lunch as I did. "How about you, Jennifer? What do you think of liver nuggets?"

She brushed back her permed hair. It's blonde like Alison's, but that's not the natural color. "I'm too excited to eat," she said. "I'm thinking about my project for the science fair."

"What are you going to do?" Winfred asked.

She stuck her nose in the air. "It's a secret. If I told you, you might copy it."

"Is it something that's going to blow up?" Tony wondered aloud.

"What? Blow up? Why would I make something that blew up?"

"I was thinking about making a project that blew up," Tony explained. "You got to get a good mark if you blow something up, right?"

"Maybe you should think of another idea," I suggested. "Something less . . . violent."

Tony shrugged. "I don't see anything wrong

with blowing something up. They blow stuff up in science."

"It may not be what my dad has in mind," I said.

I met Alison by her locker after lunch. "How was choir?" I asked.

"The usual," she answered. "How was Mrs. Bawlf's lunch?"

"It's getting worse," I declared as I rooted for my books in my locker. I told her about the liver nuggets and the quahog-burgers, and how I'd been rude to Mrs. Bawlf.

"Your dad will be upset when she tells him," Alison said sympathetically.

"I know. If he wasn't my father, what's the worst that would happen? Maybe I'd get a day in detention. When he finds out, he's going to give me a detention at school, plus ground me for the weekend at home. No other kid in the whole school has to put up with that."

"Sarah does."

Sarah is my eight-year-old sister.

"She's only in third grade," I said. "She's too young to know any better. She thinks it's neat to have her Daddy at school."

"I agree with her," Alison said. "It's not that awful. In a way, you're lucky to have your dad so close. I won't get to see my father until I visit

11

him at Christmas. I wish he weren't so far away."

Alison's folks split up a couple of years ago. Her father moved to Dunedin, Florida.

"You're the one who's lucky," I pointed out. "You get to go someplace warm for Christmas and spring break. I'd give anything to get away from winter."

"I'd rather have my dad all the time," she said softly.

The bell rang, and I closed my locker. There was no way I was going to get any sympathy from Alison. I'd just have to stew about it on my own. Being the principal's daughter isn't fair. It just isn't.

We had a double period of English in the afternoon. English is my favorite subject. I really like my teacher, Mr. Manning.

"All right, everyone," Mr. Manning said at the beginning of class. "We're going to set up sharing partners for creative writing. You're going to read your writing to a partner."

"You mean a story buddy," Steve said. "That's what Mrs. Reid called it in third grade."

"More or less," Mr. Manning said.

Alison put up her hand. "Do we get to choose our own partners?" she asked.

Mr. Manning shook his head. "That sounds like a loaded question." He smiled. "This time, I think you should work with somebody else. You and

Marcie are partners for everything."

"Awww," Alison and I groaned together.

"Don't make her my partner," Steve called out.

Mr. Manning gave him the teacher-stare. "You know, Steven, sometimes I find your sense of humor a little trying."

I figured that was a nice way of saying, "Stick a sock in it, jerkface."

"Alison, you can share your stories with Jennifer," Mr. Manning went on. "And, Marcie, I think you'll work well with Eric.

Eric, I thought. Eric Stenson? Oh, no.

Alison gave me a sympathetic look.

"Winfred, you can share with . . ." Mr. Manning continued, but I didn't listen to him.

I was sort of shell-shocked. Eric Stenson?

I noticed Eric looking at me. He made a gentle smile as if he were saying, "Sorry you got stuck with me."

My father calls Eric an underachiever. That's teacher-talk for a student who might fail his grade.

After Mr. Manning finished pairing everyone up, he said, "Get your creative writing folders and find a place in the room where you can read to each other. If you'd like to rearrange the desks, feel free."

Eric and I found a spot at the work table in the back of the room. We turned the chairs so we were facing each other.

"It's too bad you can't share with Alison," he told me.

Yes it is, I thought. "It's all right," I said.

This was the first time I'd spoken to Eric since school started. He'd been really quiet this year. Not like sixth grade. He's Steve's best friend, and last year he had been a Butz clone. One day, while we were waiting in line for recess, Eric had snapped the back strap of my training bra through my sweatshirt.

"You complete, utter, absolute lunkhead," I'd said.

But he hadn't done anything like that this year. In fact, most of the time I didn't even know he was in the class.

"I know you're upset because you have to work with the class dummy," he said now.

"I don't think that," I told him.

But I felt a little guilty. That's exactly what I had been thinking.

"I want you to know that I'm really happy to be sharing with you," he said.

I didn't know what to say to that. In a way, it made me feel uncomfortable. "Why don't you read me something you wrote?" I asked.

"I don't have that much. Besides, it isn't any good. Read your stuff. I'd like to hear it."

I shuffled through my folder. "Look, Eric," I said. "I don't have many stories. Most of the things I write for creative writing are" — As soon as I said it, he was going to moan. Or laugh. Or both — "poems."

He didn't moan. Or laugh. In fact, he seemed interested.

"That's great," he said. "I can't write poems, but I like reading some of them."

"You do?"

He nodded. "Yeah, sometimes poems say things that you can't say any other way."

"I thought I was the only person in class who liked poetry," I said. "Everybody else thinks it's dopey to like poetry."

"I don't," Eric said.

"Jennifer likes poems," I said. "But she likes *everything* in school, so she doesn't count. And Winfred probably likes them as well, but it's just another chance for him to get intense, so he doesn't count, either. But I had no idea that you liked them."

He made his soft smile. It was almost like a puppy dog look. "I like to read poems," he said as he brushed back his long bangs. "It's neat to see how the writer has played with the words."

"Right," I agreed. "Sometimes I get really into a poem. You know what? I like writing them more than reading them. I'm not that good, but sometimes I feel I have to write something down in a poem."

"Does Alison like them?" he asked.

"I've tried reading some to her a few times, but

she just says, 'Interesting.' I can tell she's only being polite."

This was major weird. I was talking to Eric as if we'd been friends for a long time.

"Read me one," Eric said.

"Okay, here's one I wrote last week."

Winter

Grandmother,
It's winter.
The cold has come;
The sky has turned gray.

But the memories
of summer
must still
glow warm.
Do not give
into the cold
so quickly.

For a few moments, Eric didn't say anything. Then he smiled and said, "Wow."

"Do you understand that?"

"I think so," he said. "You're worried because your grandmother is growing old, right?"

I nodded. "She's sick, and my mom says that sometimes she finds it hard to . . . say, Eric, I don't think I've . . . I mean, Alison thought I was writing about cold weather. I didn't think . . ."

"Read me another," he said.

"Can I ask you a question first?" I said. "How come you can see what my poem is about, and you're . . . you're . . ."

"Flunking English?" he finished.

"Okay," I said.

"I don't know." He shrugged and pointed to his forehead. "When I try to write down what's in here, it comes out all jumbled. Read me another."

So I did.

And then another. And another. Every time I finished a poem, Eric told me how much he liked it. The double period flew by.

"Sharing with Jennifer is a drag," Alison told me as we changed classes. "She's so full of it, if you know what I mean. What's it like sharing with Eric?"

"Interesting," I said. "There's a side of him that nobody knows about."

She gave me a squinty-eyed stare. "What's that mean?"

"I don't really know," I said.

I play on the Fifth Street School girls volleyball team. At 3:10, I had a practice. After it was over, I was surprised to find Eric still in school and sitting on the floor in the hallway, waiting for me.

3.
Me and You?

"What are you doing sitting on the floor?" I asked Eric.

He stood up and wiped the backside of his jeans. "It's better than sitting on the ceiling. Those lights can get hot."

"That's funny," I said. "Sort of weird, but funny."

"I'm waiting for you," he told me. "You going to be long?"

"A few minutes," I said. "I just have to put on my North Pole beach outfit." I struggled into my snow pants.

"You going to wait for Alison?" Eric asked.

"She doesn't play volleyball. She's long gone," I said as I put on my sweater. "Monday is her gymnastics class."

"You getting a ride with your dad?"

I wrapped my scarf around my neck. "He went to a meeting at the school board. Besides, he's

18

mad at me. I was a little lippy to Mrs. Bawlf at lunch. He gave me a detention for tomorrow."

"Can I walk home with you, then?"

I pulled on my boots. "Walk?"

"Aren't you walking? It's a nice day."

I zipped my coat. "It's zero. How can it be a nice day when it's zero? I'm going to catch the bus."

"Can I catch the bus with you?"

I slipped on my hat. "Sure. I can't stop you getting on the bus."

"I want to talk to you about something," he said.

"I hate winter," I told him. "I hate getting dressed to go outside."

"I like your hat," he said.

"Thanks. My aunt knitted it for me. She lives in Plattsburgh, New York. They have a lot of winter there as well. My aunt calls it a toque."

"A what?"

"A toque."

"Bless you."

"Huh?"

"It sounded like you sneezed."

"You sure do have a weird sense of humor, Eric."

He smiled. "Where do you think the name *toque* comes from?"

"I don't know," I said. "But it sort of fits, doesn't it? It sounds stupid. What else would you call a big, wool sock that you wear on your head?"

"Right," he agreed. "You ever wonder where *hockey puck* came from?"

"Not really. Can we go outside?" I said. "Now that I'm dressed in forty pounds of duck feathers and wool, I'm too hot."

After I'd adjusted my earmuffs and Eric had buttoned his parka, we walked to the bus stop and waited for the bus. Fortunately, it arrived in a couple of minutes. We rode past two stops before Eric told me what was really on his mind.

"I'm really worried about the science fair thing. The way Ms. Rand explained it, it sounds like a lot of work. I mean, coming up with an idea will be hard enough. But turning the idea into a report is big league labor."

"It sure is," I agreed. "Don't forget we have to build a model or display that shows our report at work."

"All in two weeks," Eric moaned. "I'll never be able to do it. I'm already flunking science. This will dump me into the minus percent."

That made me smile. "You're so dramatic, Eric. You can't get a minus mark. You're too hard on yourself. You'll do okay."

"This is going to bury me!"

"Ms. Rand said we could work with a partner," I pointed out. "Why don't you do your project with Steve? Then you'll only have to do half the work."

"I already asked him," Eric said. "Steve doesn't

20

want to work with me. He figures I'll slow him down. He said that he wanted to win the money and if he had to work with me, there wasn't a hope in . . . in . . . you know where."

"How come you're still his friend when he says stuff like that?" I asked.

"Steve's okay. He's funny most of the time."

"It doesn't sound too funny to be shot down like that."

"What Steve says is true, though, isn't it?"

"Don't do that," I said. "If you talk that way, you're going to end up believing it. You're no different from anybody else."

"You really mean that?"

" 'Course I do. In a lot of ways, you're better. I liked working with you in English today. You're the best creative writing sharing partner in the whole class."

"You're not just saying that?"

"I wouldn't want to work with anybody else." I smiled.

The bus turned right at Tidyman's Supermarket in the mall, the stop before I got off.

I stood up to make my way to the door. "I'll see you tomorrow."

"I know you'll probably say no, but will you be my partner for the science fair?" he asked.

"Huh?"

"Will you do a science project with me?"

"Me and you?"

He nodded.

I wasn't expecting that question.

"Well, I . . . I . . . look, Eric . . ."

"That's okay. I understand. You don't want to be slowed down by someone who's failing."

The bus pulled to a stop.

"Eric, I can't. . . ."

"Hey, you standing up, are you getting off?" the bus driver called impatiently.

"I understand," he repeated.

"It's not that I . . ."

"Are you getting off?"

"Steve was right," Eric said.

"Are you getting off?"

"I'd love to be your partner," I told him, even though that was the very last thing that I wanted to say.

When I opened the door, I saw my mother bouncing in front of the TV in the family room. She comes home from the office early on Mondays and Wednesdays to exercise with *Afternoon Aerobics* on the cable channel.

"Hi, honey," she called between breaths. "How was school?"

"Okay."

"What did you learn today?" she puffed.

"Nothing."

"That's nice."

This is how my mother and I usually say hello

every weekday after school. Ever since kindergarten she's been asking me what I've learned at school, and every time I say "nothing." If she took the time to think about it, she'd realize that I haven't learned anything in eight years.

I took off my boots, hung up my coat, snow pants, and sweater, and put my mitts, hat, and scarf on the radiator. Then I went into the kitchen, helped myself to a diet Coke, and sat down at the table to think about my problem.

Why had I told Eric that I'd be his partner?

"I'm so stupid sometimes," I said to the soda can.

You know why you did it, I thought. You did it because you felt sorry for Eric. No, Eric was feeling sorry for himself, and you decided to make him feel better. That was such a nice thing to do.

"But so stupid," I whispered.

Stupid because Alison already thinks she and I are partners. We always are. When she finds out I'm going to work with Eric, she'll go snake on me. She'll think I've deserted her. She's like that. She'll go snake.

"I thought I heard you talking," Mom said as she walked into the kitchen. She mopped her face with a paper towel and grabbed the juice pitcher from the refrigerator.

"I was just kicking myself for something I did."

Mom got a glass from the cupboard and poured a large oj. "Sounds serious."

"It is. I agreed to be Eric Stenson's partner for the science fair."

"The science fair?"

"Didn't Dad tell you?"

"You know he never mentions what's going on at school unless I ask him."

So I had to tell her. "And I agreed to be Eric's partner."

"And?"

"And that's it."

"That doesn't sound like much of a problem."

"It is. Alison will be really upset when I tell her about Eric."

Mom took a long swallow of oj. "Don't be silly," she said. "Just tell her that you want to work with somebody else for a change. She'll understand."

"This is Alison McBride we're talking about," I said. "This is the same girl who avoided me for a whole week in fourth grade because I was chosen as Wendy for the class play, *Peter Pan*. That was the part she wanted."

"And that was three years ago," Mom pointed out.

"This is the same girl who wouldn't speak to me for seven whole days because I sat next to the teacher on the school bus when we went to Glacier Park. That was last year in sixth grade."

"I was speaking to Mrs. McBride at PTA last week," Mom said. "She was telling me how Alison is maturing."

"She'll still go snake."

"Go snake?"

"She'll be like Tony's science project."

"You're not making any sense, Marcie."

"I don't want to talk about it anymore," I grumbled.

Mom studied me for a few seconds. "All right, then. Let me tell you my news. Guess what happened at work today?"

I've always thought questions like that are stupid. The only answer that makes any sense is another question.

"What?" I said.

I wasn't expecting anything interesting. Mom is a lawyer, but not the exciting kind. She doesn't deal with criminals and court cases. She doesn't even do mildly interesting things like divorces. She's a real estate lawyer. She does paperwork when people buy a house.

"I closed a property deal in town for a client today. This gentleman just happens to be one of the owners of Marmot Basin Ski Resort," Mom told me. "Do you know where that is?"

"Someplace cold?"

"It's in Canada. In the Rocky Mountains, near a place called Jasper."

"Someplace cold," I said.

"Anyway, the client gave me a week-long pass for spring break in March, as a token of appreciation for my hard work."

"Whoopee," I said sarcastically.

"It's for six people," Mom explained. "Hotel and lift tickets and meals. You'll be able to take Alison. And Sarah can take Denis."

"Whoa." I held up my hands. "I'm not going to take anybody because I'm not going anywhere."

Mom put her juice on the counter and folded her arms across her chest. "Yes, you are, young lady. I've decided to make sure that you become more active. I don't want you to grow up to be a couch potato."

"Mother!" I started to protest. "Don't you think you're being a little silly here? I *am* active. I like gym. I play on the volleyball team. It's just that I don't like cold weather. I've told you a thousand times. I don't want to go skiing because you have to do it someplace cold."

"I think it's an awful waste," Mom said. "We have some of the best skiing in the whole world in this state. And you won't take advantage of it. Why won't you try it again? You used to like it when you were smaller."

"That's before I knew better. That's when you *made* me go. Now I'm old enough to know that freezing my buns on the side of a mountain is not my idea of a good time."

"Well, this time I don't care what you say, Marcie," she said. "This time I'm going to be firm. It'll be a great week, and you're going."

"But . . ."

"But nothing," she said as she left the kitchen.

"Well, that cheered me up," I said to the diet Coke.

Don't panic, Marcie, I thought. March is half a year away. There're lots of things you can do to make Mom change her mind before then. There're lots of ways to get out of it.

Trouble was, I was going to have to think of one.

4.
Bugging Time
and REGET

My father *insists* on a family supper. We always have a sit-down meal, and we're never allowed to watch TV while we eat.

Dad says, "Such stuff is the glue for good family relationships. The family that meets and eats, never competes."

I don't really know what that means.

During supper we take turns talking about our day. It's our Bugging Time. Bugging Time is my mother's version of a Great Idea. We tell each other about our day. And if we want to, we get to tell the rest of the family what's bugging us. That's how it got its name.

Sarah always goes first. We spend the first few minutes of Bugging Time listening to her tell us that we never listen to her, that we're never interested in what she has to say.

In a way, I guess she's right. The stuff she talks about is usually boring, like what she's doing in third grade. Nothing exciting ever happens in third grade. Besides I've already done it. If her stories aren't boring, they're dumb, like the one about the time machine that Denis built in his basement.

Denis is Sarah's friend, and one of Alison's two brothers. He's in Sarah's third-grade class.

"That's great about the crayon art, Suds," I said when she was finished. "And that time machine is really interesting."

Suds is Sarah's pet name. She got it because she dumped a whole box of Mr. Bubble into the tub when she was little. We had to rent one of those water vacuum cleaners to suck up all the foam.

"You never listen," she whined. "I said we were drawing with pastels."

"Same thing." I smiled at her.

"No, it isn't."

"Can I go now?" I asked her. "You finished?"

"Pastels aren't crayons."

"Can I go now?" I repeated.

She started to pout, so I took my turn.

I think Mom was ready to be attacked for her ski week idea, but I didn't even mention it. I had a hundred plus days to handle that problem.

Instead, I complained about Mrs. Bawlf and the strange lunches.

"Well, I'm certainly glad you brought that up," Dad said. "Because you're grounded for this weekend."

My mother looked puzzled. "What does a liver nugget have to do with Marcie being grounded?"

So my dad told her about what had happened at lunch. Only the way he explained it, it sounded as if I'd told her to go jump off Niagara Falls or something just as terrible.

"Marcie!" Mom scolded.

I tried to explain what really had happened, and how the weird food was so awful that I couldn't help myself. "And it's not fair that I'm grounded for something I already got a detention for. Nobody in the whole school would get punished twice for the same thing. It only happens to me because I'm Marcie Wilder, and my dad is Mr. Wilder, the principal."

"Marcie!" Mom said as if she hadn't heard me. "How could you be so rude?"

"I just explained that," I said.

"Speaking to Mrs. Bawlf that way is simply not acceptable," Mom said.

"You didn't listen to me," I complained.

"Join the club," Sarah grumbled.

"It's finished," Dad said sternly. "Is there anything else you wish to say about another subject?"

I was so angry that I bit my lip until it hurt. If I said what I was feeling, I'd be grounded for next weekend as well. Heck, if I said what I was feeling, I'd be grounded for the next thirty years.

So, I took a deep breath and started bugging

about the science fair, about how I thought it was going to end in disaster.

"That's silly," my father said. "Nothing can go wrong."

"You've said that before, and stuff has gone wrong."

"But this is an excellent idea," Dad pointed out. "Not only is it good for school spirit, but it's a terrific class assignment."

"Tony Alfredo is going to make something that blows up," I warned. "I'm serious. You don't know my classmates like I do. It's not just Tony. It's a feeling."

"Well, your feeling is incorrect this time," Dad asserted in his principal voice. "I'm quite excited about the science fair. So is Mrs. Bompas at the school board. Even Alison told me that she was looking forward to it."

The mention of my friend's name made me realize I had a more immediate problem. I was going to have to tell her about Eric and me after supper.

I went to the bathroom before going over to Alison's. The toilet paper was almost finished, so I opened the cupboard under the sink to grab another roll.

That's when I saw it.

It was placed behind the toilet paper, hidden from view: a skinny, long, black bottle with a

31

spray top. I'd never seen anything like that before. It was too tiny to be hairspray, too small to be deodorant. I reached in and picked it up.

"REGET," the label read. "For the treatment of MPB. Use only when prescribed by a physician. Read enclosed instructions for possible side effects."

Taped to the side was a drugstore label. It was dated two weeks ago and said, "Grigg Wilder. Use twice a day, as directed. Dr. F. Gagesch." She's our family doctor.

"Dad must be sick," I said to myself.

He didn't seem sick. Surely he would have told us if he were. But we keep our medicine in the cabinet over the sink. Why was this REGET stuff hidden behind the toilet paper? He wouldn't have put it there unless he wanted it to be a secret.

What was REGET, anyway?

"Where are you going?" Dad asked as I got my coat from the closet.

"Alison's," I said. "I already told Mom. Dad, are you feeling okay?"

"I feel fine. Why?"

"Are you really fine?"

"I just said that. Why are you asking?"

"Oh, no reason. I'm curious. I was wondering when the last time you saw Dr. Gagesch was, that's all."

He shrugged. "I don't know. A couple of years

ago. Why are you asking me this?"

"I'm curious," I repeated. "You know how you and Mom were talking about health insurance the other day? How you weren't getting your money's worth because nobody in our family gets sick?"

He nodded. "But we still need health insurance. You can never tell what will happen," he said. "If one of us gets seriously ill, it would cost thousands and thousands of dollars."

That didn't ease my worry. Why was he hiding something from me? The label proved he'd seen the doctor two weeks ago.

Was he so ill that he didn't want to tell us?

This was weird. My dad never lied.

As I grabbed my scarf, mittens, and toque, I thought about wasting another ten minutes of my life. I figure that's how long it takes me to get dressed in my winter clothes.

White Falls is so far north that we've already had a month of winter by Thanksgiving.

As I was putting on my Montana survival outfit, I did a little math in my head to help take my mind off the REGET and my meeting with Alison.

In White Falls, it's winter for half the year, deep winter from December to March. That's four months, or about one hundred and twenty days. I get dressed and undressed in my outside clothes twice a day, on average. So that's about a half hour's worth of on-and-off a day. A half hour times one hundred and twenty days is sixty hours.

If I put that another way, I spend twelve hours a day for nearly a whole week putting on and taking off my winter clothes. Multiply that by twelve years and I've spent three whole months of my life putting on hats and boots and stuff.

Arrrggghhh!

I walked over to Alison's house. Despite the cold, I took my time. I knew I had to tell her about Eric, but I didn't want to. She wasn't going to understand.

I rang the bell, and Denis let me in.

"Hi, guy," I said as I unzipped my coat and loosened my scarf. "How are you?"

"Great." He grinned. "I got a new invention."

"I heard. Sarah told us you built a time machine in the basement."

"That's right," he said. "Only I can't get it to work. I sent Batman into the future, but I can't bring him back."

"You sent your poodle into the future?" It was hard for me not to smile.

"Yeah," he nodded. "I thought I'd try it on the dog first. But I don't think I had the dial set right. I may have sent him anyplace in the house. I can't bring him back 'cause I don't know where he landed. I'm worried about him. What am I going to tell my mom?"

"Kind of hard to explain that you sent your pet

into the future, isn't it?" I like playing along with Denis. He's so weird that he's very entertaining. "How long ago did you send him into the future?"

"I don't know for sure." He shrugged. "The dial just turns. It doesn't really count. Not long, though. Just a few minutes into the future."

"Then there's no need to worry. He's going to show up soon, isn't he?"

He thought about that. "Gosh, I didn't think of that. Thanks, Marcie. I feel a lot better now. You want to come take a look at my machine?"

"Maybe some other time," I told him. "I've got to talk to Alison about something important."

He pointed up the stairs. "She's in her room."

"Thanks," I said.

Here we go, I thought.

5.
Best Friends, Right?

I climbed the stairs and tapped on Alison's door. "It's me," I called.

She let me in. "Close my door, Marcie," she said. "I have to get changed for my figure skating lessons, and I don't want Karl peeking in. He's turned into a peeping Tom."

Karl is Alison's other brother. He's only four years old.

Alison removed her plush animals from her chair so I could sit down. I took off my coat and tossed it on the bed.

"It's so bizarre," Alison said. "Karl has got this thing for underwear all of a sudden. It seems that underwear is the big joke at his play school right now. You just have to say underwear, and he has a laughing fit. He has some kind of bet with one of his friends. Whoever sees the most people in their underwear in one week wins. Isn't that perverted? Four-year-olds are so strange. I can't remember being fascinated by underwear."

I could. I used to think it was pretty funny in preschool.

"Anyway, what's up?" she asked as she slipped off her jeans. "How come you're here? I don't have too much time. My lesson starts at 7:30."

"You ever hear of something called REGET?" I asked.

"REGET? What is it?"

"Some kind of drug."

"A drug? Why would I know anything about drugs?"

"This is a drug you get from the doctor," I told her. "Something you take if you've got MPB. Something you spray."

"A drug that you spray? You mean like that nose stuff?"

"I don't think so. The bottle is too big, and the sprayer thing wouldn't fit up your nose."

"What's MPB?"

"I don't know," I said. "I thought you might have heard about it."

She shook her head. "Sorry. Is that why you came over?"

I shook my head and took a deep breath. "No. It's something else."

"What?"

"You and I are best friends, right?"

"Sure," she said. "Always and forever. Why?"

"Well, best friends can tell each other anything. And best friends always try to be understanding, don't they? Like about sitting next to a teacher on the bus."

She didn't catch on. She turned around so I could zip up her skating costume. "Before you go on, tell me how much you like my new outfit."

"It's kind of skimpy," I said.

"That's the style right now."

"Then it looks nice," I told her.

"Thanks. The skating show is on Saturday, and I'm getting a little nervous. You're still going to come and watch me, aren't you?"

"I can't anymore," I told her. "My dad grounded me for the weekend because of what I said to Mrs. Bawlf."

"The whole weekend?"

"It isn't fair, is it?"

She didn't answer my question. "My dad called last night. He's already got our plane tickets for the Christmas holidays. We fly out the afternoon before Christmas Eve."

"Sounds terrific," I said. "Can I go, too?"

She stared at me for a few seconds. "Would your folks let you? They'd want you home for Christmas, wouldn't they?"

"It won't hurt to ask," I said. "I'll plead and beg. I'll ask for the plane ticket as my Christmas gift."

"That would be wonderful." Alison smiled. "Why didn't I think of that? My dad wouldn't mind. He's got a huge house. We could go to Disney World. It's only about an hour from Dunedin."

"It's hot there, right?"

"It's warm," she said. "At least, there's no snow."

"I love it already. I'll ask my parents. Maybe I can trade Christmas for skiing."

"What?"

"If I agree to something my mom wants, maybe she'll agree to something I want," I said.

"Whatever." She smiled. Alison didn't have a clue what I was talking about. "About the skating. If you can't come on Saturday, you can watch the dress rehearsal on Thursday night. Why don't you come then?"

"I'll be there."

"Thanks. Now what was all that stuff about friendship?"

"Well." I took another deep breath. "You know this science fair project . . ."

"I've already been thinking about it," she said. "I think we should do something on electricity. My mom says she can help us make all these experiments with batteries and lights and bells and things. How does that sound?"

"It sounds real good." I nodded. "For you."

"If you have a better idea for us, I'm willing to listen. Is that what you meant about friends being understanding?"

"Not quite. . . ."

Alison placed her finger on her lips to *sssh* me.

39

Then she leaned her head in the direction of her door. An angry scowl creased her face.

In a determined tiptoe, she marched to the door and flung it open. Her brother Karl almost fell into the room. He'd had his face pressed against the thin crack between the door and the molding. He'd been spying through the tiny space.

"You little grunge!" Alison yelled.

"I saw your underwear." Karl giggled as he ducked her punch and ran to the safety of his room.

"I'm going to rip out your lungs!" she shouted after him. Then she stomped back into her room. "You're so lucky you don't have to put up with that."

She went to her closet to get her skates. "Where were we, Marcie?"

"The science project."

"Right. I was just about to be an understanding friend and let you tell me a better idea for our project."

I made a *tutting* sound as I searched for the right words. The best thing to do was to come right out and tell her the truth. "Alison," I said, "I . . ."

"Ruff! Ruff!"

We both jumped.

Batman came charging around Alison's bed, threw his front paws on my lap, and started licking my face.

"Batman! Get down!" Alison scolded. "What are you doing upstairs? Bad dog!"

She grabbed the poodle's collar to pull him away and dragged him to the doorway.

"Go downstairs," she ordered.

The dog scampered away.

"That's strange," she said. "He never comes upstairs. How come we didn't notice him before?"

"The time . . ." I stopped.

"The time what?"

What was I thinking of? An eight-year-old couldn't make a time machine. That was impossible. There weren't such things as time machines. "Maybe he was hiding because he knew he shouldn't be here," I said.

"I guess." She glanced at her clock. "I really have to get to my skating lesson. I'll call you later about our science project."

I had to tell her now. I didn't want to wait until later.

"Look, Alison, I *want* to be your partner for the science fair, but I *can't* be your partner."

"Pardon?"

"You heard it the right way."

She sat down on her bed. "Now I have time," she said. "This is more important than my figure skating lesson. Why *can't* you be my partner?"

"Because . . . er . . . because . . . this is so hard, Alison. I can't be your partner because I've agreed to do the science project with Eric."

41

Her back went stiff. "With Eric?"

"I can explain. . . ."

"Marcie," she stopped me. "You don't have to do that. I understand."

"You do? You're not going to go snake?"

"We're in seventh grade now. I'm not going to get angry. I told you, I understand. You like Eric more than you like me."

"That's stupid, and you know it. You see, it started in English today. I was sharing my poems with Eric, and . . ."

"Eric is a jerk," she said.

"That was last year. He's different. You should have heard some of the things he said about my poems."

"He listens to your dumb poetry, so you think he's better than me."

"Of course not . . . *dumb poetry?* What do you mean *dumb poetry?* Why did you say that?"

"Because it's true."

"That hurts, Alison."

"How do you think I feel, Marcie? Think about what you've just done to me. How do you think it feels when my best friend tells me she's going to work with someone else."

"Maybe it's like Mr. Manning said. Maybe we need to do stuff with different people."

That was the wrong thing to say.

"Fine," Alison said. "Since you've already chosen Eric over me, we don't have anything else to talk about. And I have to leave. I want you to go."

"You *are* going snake, aren't you? You're just doing it in a quiet way."

"Go write another stupid poem so your stupid boyfriend can go google over it."

"Okay," I said. "I don't want to stay if you're going to say nasty things."

"Maybe we can say hello at school," she said. "If you're not too busy with Eric."

"Friends should be able to talk to each other." I stood up and took my coat. "You're not being reasonable."

"I wouldn't have done anything like this to you, Marcie. And if I'd even thought about it, I'd have told you before I agreed to be partners with somebody else. Now please go home."

I walked out of her room and met Denis on the stairs.

"You look like you're crying." he said.

I wiped my eyes. "I had something in my eye."

"Batman's back," he told me.

"He was hiding in Alison's room," I said.

Denis scratched his frizzy hair. "That's where he showed up, huh? I'll have to try to fix the dial. Thanks."

This time, I didn't feel like playing along with him.

6.
Major Confusion

It took me a long time to fall asleep that night. I worried about REGET a little. Dad couldn't be sick. He was too healthy. He'd never get great ideas if he were sick. And if he had special medicine, there'd be no need to hide it behind the extra toilet paper. Still, it was strange that he'd lied to me. That definitely wasn't Dad.

Mostly I thought about what had happened at Alison's.

I'd gone to her house knowing she'd get angry. And she did, sort of. She didn't go snakey mad, but there was no doubt that she was upset.

I'd gone to her house thinking the problem was Alison's temper. *I* hadn't done anything wrong. Alison would get upset because *she* wouldn't understand. After all, that was one of *her* faults.

She didn't understand. But maybe it wasn't her temper that was the problem. Maybe she had a good reason to be upset. Alison and I have been best friends forever. It's just natural to think we'd automatically be science project partners.

I mean, I assumed we'd be partners. How would I feel if it were reversed? What if she'd told me she was working with somebody else? I'd be upset. No matter how she'd explain it, I'd be hurt. I think. Being a best friend means you get to count on the other person. It means you know they're going to be there . . . all the time. When it's time to choose a partner for anything, it's going to be your best friend. Maybe *I* was wrong.

Then again, doesn't part of being a best friend mean you try to understand when things like this happen? Doesn't it mean you at least listen to what your friend is trying to say? Doesn't it mean you understand that your friend didn't really have a choice?

Did I have a choice? Could I have said no to Eric? How would that have made him feel? How would that have made me feel?

What about the thing she'd said about my poems? She was deliberately trying to get back at me. She said a nasty thing because she knew it would make me feel awful. It did.

She knew how I feel about my poems. Even if she didn't understand them, she knew how special they are to me. Had I hurt her enough for her to do that to me?

Talk about major confusion. How was I ever going to sort out this mess?

The last time I checked my clock, it was 1:43. I must have fallen asleep sometime after that.

My mother was partially right about Alison being more mature. This time she didn't ignore me completely. She spoke to me at school the next day. But it was just "hello," and she didn't smile. The Cold Shoulder is only one step above ignoring me completely. At lunch, she sat at a different table.

I ate with Eric, Steve, and Jennifer. Mrs. Bawlf's main course was called Pondfood Combo. We hadn't had it before. Pondfood Combo was little chunks of fishy meat mixed up with lots of noodles and a few pieces of carrot.

"Hey, Jennifer," Steve asked at one point. "What are you so happy about today? You've been walking around with a big, dumb smile on your face all morning. You're even more sickening than usual."

"Why don't you go soak your head," she answered.

My lack of sleep and my confusion about Alison and me had put me in a foul mood. So I added to Jennifer's suggestion, "In a bucket of toxic waste."

Steve acted as if he were offended. "Do your parents know you talk that way?"

"You *are* smiling a lot," Eric said to Jennifer. "Is it your birthday?"

She shook her head. "I'm just excited about my science project. It's going to be terrific."

"Not as amazing as mine," Steve declared. "Those fifty buckaroonies are as good as in my pocket."

"What's your project about, Jennifer?" Eric asked.

"She won't tell us," I grumbled. "It's a big secret. She doesn't want us copying."

"I can guess," Steve said. "She's going to do a display that tells us how she had the brain transplant with a Pop Tart."

"Did that happen to you?" I asked him.

"Aw, come on," Steve coaxed. "I'm just kidding around. I'm really curious about your project, Jennifer. Tell you what — you come to my place and show me yours, and I'll show you mine."

"You're so crude," I said.

"And you have no sense of humor," he chuckled.

"Neither do you," I replied. "Only another jerk would think you're funny."

I regretted saying that right away. Not because of Steve, but because Eric had told me that he thought Steve was funny most of the time.

Eric didn't pick up on it, though. He was curious about Jennifer's secret. "So you won't tell us what it is?" he asked her.

She thought for a moment. "Well, since you can't get the help I'm going to get, I guess it won't hurt to tell you. I'm doing my project on how to stop mosquitoes from biting. I'm going to use real mosquitoes."

"How are you going to do that? Where are you going to get a mosquito from?" Eric asked. "It's winter outside."

"Tell me about it," I said. "It's always winter outside."

Boy, there was a lot of stuff to make me miserable: the science project, Alison, the REGET puzzle, Mrs. Bawlf's food, winter, Steve Butz, my mother's ski trip, being the principal's daughter — all kinds of things.

Jennifer leaned her elbows on the table. "My dad knows all kinds of important people. He really is a wonderful person. A lot like his only daughter."

"We've heard this before," Steve said. "And we didn't believe it then. Just tell us how you're going to get a mosquito in February."

She narrowed her eyes at him. "My dad knows Dr. Ruth Calpuzzo. She's a professor at the University of Montana in Helena, and she's world-famous and . . ."

"Is there any way you can speed it up?" Steve asked.

"Do you want to hear this or not?" Jennifer snapped.

"Shut up, Steve," I said.

I was more surprised I'd said that than Steve

was. I think telling someone to shut up is rude. But Steve deserved it, and I was glad I'd said it.

"Thanks, Marcie." Jennifer smiled at me. "Anyway, Ruth, she lets me call her that, is a world-famous entomologist. I bet you don't know what that is, do you, Steve?"

I bet I don't, either, I thought.

"She did your brain transplant?" Steve smirked.

Jennifer ignored him. "She knows all about insects," she told us. "She's going to let me have some mosquitoes from her lab at the university. And she's going to tell me some ways to stop them from biting. I'm going to develop my own secret formula for a mosquito repellent. Maybe I'll become world famous for it."

I wondered if it was possible to make a Steve Butz repellent.

"That *is* good." Eric nodded. "You'll get an A plus for that."

"Of course I will," Jennifer agreed. "What other mark would I get?"

"Well, it ain't going to beat mine," Steve said.

"Okay, Mr. Hot Stuff, what are you going to do?" I asked.

"Well, last night my old man was sorting out his fishing things," Steve told us. "He's going up to Canada to do some ice fishing on the weekend."

"You're going to do your project on fishing?" Jennifer asked.

Steve shook his head. "Naw, nothing so stupid. I'm doing it on food for the future. A way to feed a hungry planet."

"Fish isn't a future food," I said. "My mother makes me eat fish now. I have a suspicion that fish is the main ingredient of Mrs. Bawlf's Pond-food Combo. Although I can't be sure."

Again, he shook his head. "Not fish," he said. "It's . . . I don't want to give it away just yet. It'll be better if it's a secret until science project day. Hey, I sound like Jennifer, don't I? I don't want to tell you 'cause I don't want you copying." Then he grabbed his throat and stuck out his tongue. "What's happening to me? I sound like Jennifer. Arrrggghhh! I've got to see a doctor real fast. I've been taken over by an alien life-force. I sound like Jennifer!"

We all ignored him.

"What are you and Alison doing, Marcie?" Jennifer asked.

"I sound like Jennifer," Steve continued. "I'm cursed. I'm possessed by a demon."

"Marcie isn't working with Alison. She's doing her science project with me," Eric said. "We're partners."

"I sound like Jenni . . . huh?!" Steve stopped and stared at Eric. Then he looked at me. "You two are partners?"

"Yeah," Eric said. "But we haven't got an idea yet."

50

"Those two are partners." Steve nodded to himself. "Well, this is news. This is sort of like getting married, isn't it? I mean, first you date, then you go steady, then you get engaged, then you become science project partners."

And that was enough. I'd had enough Steve Butz, enough winter, enough principal's daughter, enough lousy lunches, enough everything. I stood up, grabbed the plate off my tray, and dumped the pile of fish and noodles and carrots over the top of his head.

7.
Protest
and Proper

Steve was so surprised that he didn't do anything. Two wide eyes stared at me as creamy
noodles and bits of fish oozed and dripped across
his face. "Why'd you do that?" he whispered.

"What a mess," Eric said.

"Ewww," Jennifer added.

Mr. Manning was on cafeteria supervision. As
soon as I shampooed Steve with Pondfood Combo,
he sent me to the office. I could tell he was trying
really hard not to laugh. There were lots of wrin-
kles around his mouth.

My dad didn't think it was funny, though. He
shouted at me and gave me another three days'
detention. Three days!

And I knew I'd get another earful during Bugging Time.

I was right.

" . . . and to say that I'm extremely disappointed
in you is to understate my feelings. Yesterday you

were rude to Mrs. Bawlf, and today you throw food on another student. What has gotten into you, Marcie?"

"I told you this afternoon in your office, Dad," I said. "Steve Butz deserved it. He's a complete jerk."

"I don't like to hear you say that about any-body," Mom lectured.

"Here's proof, then," I went on. "Once he stuffed two kindergarten kids into a garbage can. Do you know what he said when Mr. Manning caught him?"

"What?" Mom asked.

"He said, 'No big deal. I was just curious. I wanted to see if they'd fit.' That sounds like grade-A jerk talk, to me."

"I don't remember that," Dad said.

"That's because Mr. Manning gave Steve a dictionary page to copy in class," I explained. "But I bet you remember last June when he cut a piece of carrot into the shape of a goldfish."

"Why did he do that?" Mom asked.

"He brought it to school in a jar of water," Dad told her. "Steve reached into the jar and chewed it in front of Jennifer Jensen. She thought it was a real fish."

"That's neat," Sarah said.

"That's disgusting," my mother said.

"Jennifer threw up," I concluded. "So you see, Steve Butz is a jerk and deserved what I did."

"But we're not discussing Steve Butz at this family's table. We are discussing the behavior of Marcie Wilder. You're grounded for next weekend as well," Dad said.

"That is definitely not fair!" I shouted.

"Marcie," my parents said together.

I lowered my voice and looked at Dad. "Well, it isn't. I don't think you should get to bring up something that happened in school. Something that you handled as Mr. Wilder, the principal." Then I turned to my mother. "I want to file a protest, Mom. This isn't a proper use of Bugging Time. Bugging Time is for family stuff. This is about school. You can see the difference, right?"

"I don't like the things you've said about Steve," she answered.

I slapped my hands on the kitchen table. "You're doing it again! It's just like last night. I'm trying to explain something to you, and you're not listening."

"That's what I say," Sarah added.

"There is no need to bang the dinner table," Mom threatened. "We *do* listen to you."

"No, you don't," Sarah and I said together.

"You stay out of this," Dad warned Sarah. "This is Marcie's problem."

"If you listened, then you'd understand," I pointed out. "It isn't fair that what happens at school should be brought up at Bugging time."

Dad didn't agree. "On the contrary, Bugging

Time is the chance for us to speak honestly to other members of this family. What happened at school was between a principal and a student. What's happening here is between parents and their daughter."

"There's no difference," I complained. "I don't stop being your daughter at school, and you don't stop being Dad."

"Marcie, didn't we make a deal a couple of years ago that I'd treat you as a regular student between 9:00 and 3:00 on school days?" Dad was trying to keep his voice calm, but there was a lot of static behind it. And there were little beads of sweat on top of his bald head.

"That's just pretend," I told him. "You're still my father. And that means I have to act different from every other kid in the whole school."

"Even me?" Sarah asked.

"Even you," I said. "You're still young enough to get away with things."

"I'm so young that nobody ever listens to me."

"What do you mean, Marcie?" Mom asked. "Why do you have to act different?"

"It means that I have to behave myself *all* the time. I can't make a mistake."

"I don't understand," Mom said.

"Everybody does something wrong in school once in a while. Everybody." I thought about that. "Okay, so maybe Jennifer Jensen and Winfred Falkingham don't, but everybody else does.

Everyone has a messy locker some of the time. Everyone forgets homework. Or talks when they're supposed to be working."

"What are you trying to say?" Dad asked.

"I have to be perfect all the time. If I'm not, you'll hear about it, and I'll get in deep trouble. Even if it's a little thing, the teachers will tell you. Everybody loses their temper once in a while and does something like I did today."

"What you did today was exceptional," Dad said. "This is the first time I can remember a student dumping a hot lunch over another student's head."

"But they do other things just as bad," I said. "And they don't get punished at school and then have the principal punish them at home for the same thing."

"There's a difference . . ." Dad began.

"Sure there is. The difference is that I'm your daughter. Steve deserved a hairful of Mrs. Bawlf's stupid food today. The only reason I got three days DT for it is because you're my dad."

"You have to set an example for the other students to follow," Dad explained. "How can I expect discipline from the other boys and girls if I don't get it from you? How can I ask them to behave if . . . " Dad stopped, and a sheepish expression crossed his face. "Oh, my," he said. "I'm saying that you are different, aren't I?"

"Yes, you are, Grigg," Mom agreed. "Why didn't we think of this before?"

"It isn't fair, is it?" I concluded. "That's a lot of pressure on me *every day*."

My father rubbed his temples. "You've given me something to think about. This has been an interesting conversation. You and I have to work a few things out, don't we, Marcie?"

"I love Bugging Time," Mom said. "It helps get things out in the open. It helps us solve our problems."

It was my turn to load the dishwasher after supper. Mom helped me.

"Oh, I almost forgot," I told her. "Eric Stenson is coming over tonight. We have to work on the science project."

"Eric?" Mom winked at me. "Really? A boy is coming to visit my daughter."

"What's that supposed to mean?"

She winked at me again.

"Why are you doing that?"

"I'm just teasing," she said. "It's just that I remember being in seventh grade. That's when boys started looking different to me. I had my first real boyfriend in seventh grade. Do you *like* Eric?"

"Give me a break, mother. Eric and I are doing a science project together. That's all."

"Maybe we should have our mother and daughter talk," Mom said.

"We've had it."

She nodded. "Yes, but there were a few things we went over a little quickly. Maybe you're ready for some more details."

"I probably already know it," I said.

"Still, it won't hurt. Where are you and Eric going to work on your project?"

"In my room."

"In your room?"

"We have to use my computer. Is there something wrong with that?"

Mom shook her head. "That's fine. Just make sure you leave your door open. That's proper."

Eric came over about a half hour later.

"We can work in my room," I said after he hung up his coat. "I've got a computer. It's just a cheap IBM clone, but it's okay. And I've got an old version of WordPerfect."

I led Eric down the hallway and told him to sit on my bed. I sat at my desk and turned on the computer.

"Before we start," I said. "Have you ever heard of something called REGET? Something a doctor would give you?"

"I don't think so. What's it for?"

"Something called MPB."

"What's that?"

"I don't know," I told him.

"I don't know, either," Eric said. "Is it important?"

"I'm not sure. It's something that's puzzling me."

"Why don't you look it up?" he suggested.

"Good idea," I said. "I'll do it tomorrow. Let's start our project. You got any ideas?"

"You know, I've never been inside a girl's room before," he said. "This is the first time."

"Don't you have any sisters?"

He shook his head. "I've got two stepbrothers, but they don't live at home anymore. One's in the Navy, and the other is in California. In a way, I'm like an only child."

"Must be nice."

"I don't know," he said. "I have nothing to compare it to."

"Come to think of it, I wouldn't want to be an only kid. I like my sister, Sarah. Now, what are we going to do our science thing on?"

He didn't answer. He was looking around my room, checking out my shelves of stuffed toys, my bookcase with my Gordon Korman books and every single copy of the Baby-sitters Club, my wall of framed class photos, the rock posters that I'd ripped from teen magazines, even the frilly curtains my grandmother had made for me.

"So do you like it?" I asked.

"Huh?"

"My room. Do you like it?"

"Oh, yeah." He smiled. "It's great. It's kind of pink, but it's great."

I looked around. It *was* kind of pink. The curtains, my bedspread, the flowered wallpaper were all pink. I'd known that, of course, but I'd never *noticed* it before.

"What's it like being a girl?" Eric asked.

"That's a dumb question. What am I supposed to say? It's the same as being a boy, I guess. Only a little different."

"I guess," he said. "Sometimes I wonder what I would have been like if I were born a girl. I wonder if my mom would have called me Erica. You ever wonder what you'd be like as a boy?"

I started to smile. "Yes, but you're the first person I've ever told that to."

"Why are you smiling? Do you think I'm being silly?"

"No," I said. "Far from it. I just never knew that boys thought about stuff like that."

"Oh, I'd never tell anybody else," he said. "Only you. I really like talking to you. It's so easy."

"Thanks."

We stared stupidly at each other for a few moments. Neither of us knew what to say next.

Fortunately, Mom came in with a plate of cookies and a couple of mugs of hot chocolate. "Brain food," she said.

Eric stood up when she entered. I could tell she was impressed by that. "Thanks, Mrs. Wilder," he said.

"You're most welcome." She beamed. "How's it going?"

"We're just getting started," I told her.

"Call me if you need anything. And remember to keep the door open," she said as she left.

"I'm not allowed to close my door," I told Eric. "If you were a girl, I could. But because you're a boy, I'm under strict orders to keep the door open. Mom says that's 'proper.' I don't know what she thinks we're going to be doing in here."

Eric blushed and checked out my posters again. I felt myself blush, too.

Now, that's a new feeling, I thought. Most weird. I'm going to have to write a poem about this one.

Eric must have been on my wavelength. "Do you write your poems on that computer?" he asked.

"You bet. I've got a floppy disk full. One hundred and forty-nine poems written over the past two years."

"Can you read some to me?"

"I guess so. But what about our project?"

"Read a few poems first."

That was all the encouragement I needed. An hour and a half later, I was still reading my poems.

We were so into my poems that Eric had to go home, and we still hadn't picked an idea for the science fair project.

As he was getting ready to leave, he said, "Thanks for sharing your poems with me."

"Anytime."

"And thanks for agreeing to be my science partner."

"No problem."

"Yes, it is," he said. "I know that Alison is angry at you."

"No, she isn't," I lied.

"You don't have to do that," he said. "I may be flunking seventh grade, but I'm not stupid."

8.
Understand?

The next morning, as I was about to enter the kitchen I heard a word that made me stop. *REGET*.

"I've been using REGET for two months now," Dad said to Mom. "And there's no improvement. It's getting worse."

I stopped and leaned my ear to the open doorway. I knew I shouldn't, but curiosity can kill more than cats.

"Give it a chance, Grigg," Mom said.

"It's getting worse, Sharon. I'm only thirty-seven. Things like this don't happen to men my age. They happen to old men. I'm too young."

That didn't sound good. An awful thought ran around my insides. Did Dad have something really serious? Is that why he hadn't told Sarah and me? Was he sparing us the worry?"

"It's happened," my mom said matter-of-factly.

"I can't see how expensive remedies are going to do any good. Besides, I'll like you even if you lose it all."

Lose it all? I wondered. Lose what?

"What are you doing?" Sarah asked as she came down the stairs.

"Nothing," I told her. "I was just thinking about something for a moment. Let's go eat breakfast."

"Okay." She smiled.

An unsmiling "hi" was the only word Alison offered on Wednesday. I had tried to call her on the phone Wednesday evening, but Denis had said that she'd gone to her judo lesson.

"Did she tell you to say that because she doesn't want to speak to me?" I asked.

"She's at judo," he repeated.

"Maybe I'll try later," I said. "How's the time machine?"

"Great," Denis told me. "I'm going to send Sarah into the future soon."

"She'll like that. Just make sure you bring her back. My folks will be pretty upset if she gets lost in time."

"Don't worry. I got the dial all fixed," he said.

Denis really is a neat kid.

I waited by Alison's locker at lunchtime on Thursday. She'd have to speak to me, even if it was only to order me out of the way.

"What do you want?" she asked when she saw me.

"I want to talk to you."

"I don't want to talk to you."

"Are you sure, Alison?"

She opened her locker and dumped her books. "I don't think we have anything to talk about."

"I want to explain about Eric and me working together."

"Look, Marcie, we went through this on Monday night. You made your choice. I understand. Why can't you understand that I don't want to talk to you?"

"Because we're best friends."

"We *were* best friends."

"It doesn't stop that easily," I said. "I want this 'hi hello' stuff to stop. I want to tell you things. I want to tell you what happened with my dad after I dumped the food on Steve. I want to tell you what Eric said in my room on Monday."

She raised her eyebrows. "So now you're inviting boys into your room?"

I didn't answer that. "I miss talking to you."

"Maybe you should have thought about that before you hurt me." She turned away and started walking toward the cafeteria.

"Wait," I called after her. "Tonight is the rehearsal for your skating show. On Monday you wanted me to come and watch you. Can I still come?"

She didn't stop. "Don't bother," she called over her shoulder.

Mrs. Bawlf's meal of the day was *oiseau a l'orange*. When I asked her what that meant, she said it was French for "Bird in Orange Sauce."

"Bird?" I wondered. "You mean like chicken?"

"Something like that," she told me.

Something-like-chicken? I thought. What's something-like-chicken? Seagull is something-like-chicken, if you think about it.

I was going to have to talk to Dad about the menu again.

I sat at a table with Eric, Winfred, and Jennifer.

"We have to get moving on our project," I said to Eric. "It's due next Friday, and we don't have a clue what we're going to do."

"Why don't you come over to my place tonight?" he suggested.

"No, thanks. You live halfway across town. I don't want to walk in the cold."

"How about we meet at the mall, then? It's only a short walk from your place. I'll treat you to a Blizzard at the Dairy Queen, and we can brainstorm ideas."

"I don't eat ice cream in the middle of winter," I said. "I have this spiritual thing about it."

"TacoTime then," he said. "Mexi-Fries with hot salsa ketchup."

That didn't sound bad. "Okay, I'll meet you there at seven. I might be a little late."

"You don't want me to call on you?" he asked.

"No, I have to go watch Alison skate."

That made him smile. "You guys are talking to each other, then?"

I shook my head. "No. She's still angry at me."

Winfred interrupted us. "Are you going to eat your lunch?" he asked me. "You haven't touched it. I wouldn't mind a little more of that delicious meat."

"The something-like-chicken?" I said. "It's that good, is it? Let me think about it for another minute, Winny. If I can't get up the courage, it's yours."

"Thanks, Marcie."

"How's your project coming, Winfred?" Eric asked.

"Pretty good," he said. "I'm building a miniature model of a working sewage disposal plant. Did you know that scientific technology saves us from drowning in our own liquid and solid wastes?"

"Ewww," Jennifer said. "I don't want to hear about that. I don't even want to think about that. That's yucky."

"Well, maybe you should think about it," Winfred said. "Just because you flush something out of sight doesn't mean that it's gone. It goes to the sewage plant. It becomes a problem for science and nature to take care of."

"Flush it!?" Jennifer scrunched up her face. "Yuck!"

"Maybe we should talk about something else," I said.

Winfred went on as if he hadn't heard our objections. "Let's all take a minute to think about sewage. Let's think of the stuff we flush down the toilet. Let's think about where it goes, and how fortunate we are to have adequate sewage disposal technology."

"Ewww!"

"Enough, Winfred!" I snapped. "We don't want to think about toilets and sewage and . . . stuff."

"Ignoring it doesn't mean we don't have to deal with it," Winfred said seriously.

"Let's not deal with it over lunch, though," Eric said.

I'd almost forgotten Mrs. Bawlf's rapidly cooling lunch. I inspected the something-like-chicken in orange sauce. For some reason, my mind put *oiseau a l'orange* and sewage into the same thought. I passed my food to Winfred.

"Thanks, again," he said. "But I'm becoming a little concerned about your diet, Marcie. I've noticed that you don't eat very much at lunch."

Steve sauntered over to our table and sat down opposite Jennifer.

"Hey, Jennifer, you want to go to the show with me tomorrow night?" he asked.

"Huh?" She looked like an invisible truck had just run over her foot.

"How about it?" he went on. "We can go see the *Friday the 13th* Festival. We can sit in the back row and watch the high school kids kiss. Maybe we can try it as well."

That invisible truck ran over her other foot. "What? Why would I want to do that? Yuck! I'd rather eat worms," she said.

"Really?" he said. "You'd rather eat worms? You know, I might be able to arrange that."

"Flushing! Worms!" That invisible truck was backing up for another run. "What a terrible lunch!" Jennifer made quick work of leaving our table.

"Don't look so stunned," Steve said to us. "I wouldn't take her to the show, and I'd never kiss her. I only said it because I knew it would bug her."

Then he looked at me. "I'm going to get back at you for the other day. But I'm going to wait until I can think of something real good. Something that will embarrass you something fierce."

"No, you're not!" Eric almost shouted at his friend. "You were asking for that on Tuesday. You do anything to Marcie, and it'll be the same as doing it to me. Understand?"

Steve wasn't expecting that. For a few seconds he just stared at Eric. Then he said, "Hey, good buddy, chill the flames."

"Understand?"

Steve looked at me. "It's cool," he said.

As we walked back to our lockers after lunch, I said to Eric, "You don't have to stick up for me, you know. I can take care of myself."

"I didn't mean to be too pushy," he said. "Steve doesn't know when to stop sometimes."

"I can stand up for myself, but it was nice of you to do it. Thanks."

"We're friends," he said. "Friends do stuff like that."

You're right, I thought. And that's why I'm going to Alison's rehearsal tonight.

I went into the school library before afternoon homeroom and found a book called *Family Health Guide*. It explained all kinds of diseases, but it didn't have a listing for MPB. Maybe Dad had something really rare.

I did find a reference to MPB, though. There was a list of drugs in the back of the book, so I looked up REGET. It said, "For treatment of MPB, see Miminatol."

So I looked up Miminatol, and it said, "A tranquilizer used to treat severe mental disorders."

Mental disorders? Was my father going insane?

9.
Crying
and Laughing

When I arrived at the arena, the kindergarten-age kids were rehearsing their number. I guess it was supposed to be *Alice in Wonderland*. There was somebody in a Mad Hatter costume, another person dressed as the Cheshire Cat, the Queen of Hearts, and so on. But there wasn't a story to it. Everybody just went onto the ice, bumped into each other, and fell over. It was a disaster.

But at the same time, it was sort of cute. I could imagine what it would be like on Saturday afternoon. All the parents would be laughing and clapping because their little kid fell on her rear end.

There were a few parents watching the dress rehearsal, but not many, maybe a dozen. Instead of sitting with them at center ice, I found a seat in the far corner. I didn't want Alison to see me.

Kids Sarah's age were next. They had a group thing where everyone was dressed as a *Star Trek* character. Then there were a couple of girls doing solos, and a boy and girl who did an ice dance.

I noticed Alison tightening her skates on one of the hockey benches, waiting for her turn.

After the couple had finished, they dimmed the lights. Alison skated to center ice, held her hands above her head like a ballet dancer, and a spotlight turned on. The speakers crackled, and a marching song blared through the almost empty seats.

And for the next two and a half minutes, she was beautiful. The way her new costume caught the lights made her look like a princess. And she'd sprayed sparkles in her hair so that it danced with blonde, twinkling waves as she moved.

Her skating was just as gorgeous. I don't know what you call those loops and jumps and twirls, but she flowed from one to another without a stumble. She looked like I wanted my poems to sound.

When the music stopped, and Alison made a bow to the few people in the audience, I discovered I was holding my breath.

She skated off the ice, and a teenage couple started a dance routine. They were pretty good, but I figured I'd better get to the mall to meet Eric. I was already a few minutes late.

I was surprised to find Alison waiting by the exit door, still dressed in her outfit. She looked more puzzled than angry. "What are you doing here?" she asked.

"I thought you wouldn't see me. I tried to sit in the furthest corner."

"When there're only ten people in the whole arena, you notice them all."

It was weird talking to her. As I said, we're the same height and on the same eye level. But her skates made her about four inches taller. It was strange looking up at her.

"Well, what are you doing here?"

"I came to watch you," I said.

"But I told you not to bother."

"I know you did. And if you tell me that a few more times, I might start to believe it. But right now you're still my best friend, and I wanted to watch you."

"You came here even after I've been so rude to you?"

"Maybe you had a reason to be rude."

"And maybe not," she said. "Maybe I was just acting stupid."

"We've done this before," I said. "Remember *Peter Pan* in fourth grade?"

She cringed. "I was such a baby about that."

"Or when I sat next to Mrs. O'Keeffe on the bus ride to Glacier Park last year?"

"Do you have to bring that up?"

"Well, this time you're not ignoring me completely. So maybe this time isn't as bad."

"I still don't understand why you came tonight," she said.

"I told you. I wanted to watch you. You see, I hope that you'll start talking to me soon. I hope everything will be normal again. And when it is, I want to be able to say that I saw you skate. I want to share it with you. I want to tell you how beautiful you looked."

"You really think so?"

I nodded. "You were great."

"Oh, Marcie, I'm glad you came to watch."

"That's what best friends do." I smiled.

And then we were both hugging each other and crying and laughing, which was sort of weird because she was on skates and taller than me.

"I've been so childish," she sobbed and giggled.

I wasn't going to argue with that.

"But it really hurt when you said you were working with Eric," she went on. "That's why I said that mean thing about your poems. I didn't want to. I don't really think that. It just came out because I was angry."

"We can talk about it now," I chuckled and wept.

We hugged for a few more seconds. "I'm going to get changed, and we'll walk home together," she said. "You can come to my place. I've been dying to hear what Steve said to you after you dumped the food on his head."

"I can't," I told her. How will she take this? I thought? "I have to meet Eric. We haven't even chosen a topic for our project yet."

She pulled away from me and, for an instant, looked like she was going to get angry again. But it passed, and she smiled at me while wiping her eyes.

And then I got a great idea of my own. "Alison, when I meet Eric, why don't I tell him that all three of us are working together? We'll ask Ms. Rand to let us be a partnership of three. I'm sure she won't mind."

"You think so? That would be great. What about Eric?"

"What boy would pass up the chance to work with two great girls like us?" I said.

Then we hugged each other again, and laughed and cried some more.

Making up with Alison made me feel warm all over. That's a hard thing to feel in Montana in November.

I walked into the mall and headed for TacoTime. As I was passing the pet store, Winfred came charging out and almost knocked me over.

"Whoa there, Winny," I said.

"I'm sorry, Marcie," he apologized. "I'm in a hurry to get back to my science project. I was just buying some aquarium filter wool. I'm going to use it to strain the sewage."

"Winny," I said. "Can I give you some advice?"

"Sure." He looked puzzled.

"This sewage thing you're doing. I think you

should find something else. I don't think it's a good idea."

"Why not?"

"Didn't you notice the way Jennifer acted when you were telling us about it at lunch?"

"But Jennifer always acts that way."

"That's right," I agreed. "You know that Mrs. Bompas is going to be a judge at the science fair, right?"

Winfred nodded. "And your father."

"Well, Mrs. Bompas sort of strikes me as a grown-up Jennifer Jensen. Can you see what I'm trying to say?"

Winfred pulled at his bottom lip as he thought. "You're saying that Mrs. Bompas will think the same way about my miniature sewage disposal plant as Jennifer does."

"You got it. And that means you don't win, and you get a lousy mark, too."

"But it's such an important concept," he said. "Without adequate sewage treatment . . ."

"Hey, you don't have to convince me. But some people, like Mrs. Bompas and my dad, might not think it's . . . um . . . *proper* for the Fifth Street School Science Fair. They might not see it the same way we do. Can you afford to chance that?"

"Maybe you're right," he said.

"I *know* I'm right."

"I've already been working on it for three days, though."

"You've got a whole week," I said. "I'm sure you can think of something else. Something better."

"Well, I do have another excellent idea."

"Great!" I slapped his arm. "Go for it."

"Ow," he rubbed his muscles.

"Sorry about that."

"I'd better get home and get started on my new project. Thanks for pointing out those facts to me, Marcie."

"Don't mention it." I smiled. "Oh, before you go, answer a question for me. In this little sewage plant, what were you going to use as the stuff?"

"As the sewage?"

I nodded.

"Real, untreated waste. Why?"

"Where were you going to get . . . no, I don't want to know."

I walked into TacoTime. No Eric. I checked my Timex digital that Grandpa Gordon had given me for my twelfth birthday. I was only a half hour late, and I'd told him that I might get there after seven. Where was he?

"Hey!" the teenager behind the counter called. "You Marcie?"

"Yes," I said.

He adjusted his paper hat. "I thought so. He told me to look for a fox with brown hair and dark eyes. I'm supposed to give you a message from this guy Eric. He said he got tired of sitting here looking at me, so he's gone to the arcade."

"Thanks," I said. "What did you mean, *a fox*?"

"It means you're good-looking." The teenager winked.

"Is that what Eric said?"

The teenager nodded. "That's how I was supposed to recognize you. You're a little young, but you'll be okay in a few years."

"You think so?"

He nodded.

I felt pretty dumb all of a sudden. What a stupid thing to ask somebody who slung burritos at TacoTime, some dopey teenager I didn't even know.

I wasn't sure how I felt about being called a fox. It was nice to know that Eric thinks I'm good-looking. But calling somebody a fox is sort of an insult, isn't it? What's that word we used in social studies class? It's sexist, isn't it? I was going to have to talk to Mom about this.

Arcade World was only two stores from TacoTime, and I found Eric at the GORF OUT machine.

"I got your message," I said.

"I was wondering if you'd forgotten about me," he said as he moved the controls. "I've caught two thousand gorfs so far. Last game I had over five thousand. I'm king of the gorfers."

I watched Eric play for a few minutes. He finished with exactly 3,886 captured gorfs.

"Not bad, huh?" he bragged.

"You ever wonder what a gorf is?" I asked him. "You ever think why you'd want 3,886 gorfs anyway?"

"Not really. You want to play?"

"No, thanks. I'm not that good at video games. Everything happens so fast that I die right away."

"This one's pretty simple," he told me. "Whoever made up the program divided the screen into a four-by-four grid. That means that a gorf can appear at any one of sixteen different points. The computer picks a random point, and you try to catch the gorf before it disappears. But it's not completely random during the first two rounds. To make sure that you get your fifty cents' worth, the computer will pick a random point next to the last gorf. That means you can narrow it down to three or four points and be ready to pounce."

"What are you talking about? How do you know that?"

"Computer games are easy when you take a few minutes to figure out how the program was made. It's just math."

"Just math? Don't you go to the resource room for extra math help? How come you can understand this computer game stuff when you can't add fractions?"

He shrugged. "I don't know. Computer games

are more interesting, I guess. I want to know how they work. I like to see how they've been programmed. I've been working on my own game in computer club. It's sort of a maze game. I've been working on it since last fall. It's taken me that long because the only language the computer knows is BASIC, and . . ."

"Is your game almost finished?" I asked.

"It is finished. I'm going to add a few more colors, but you can play it."

"That's it," I told him. "That's it! That's what our science fair project should be."

10.
Gorf out
and MPB

"Our science project should be my game?" Eric asked.

"Sure," I said. "Why not? There's nothing more scientific than a computer, is there? We'll show your game. I'll write up what you did in a booklet. Alison can make a poster and do artwork for the cover. She's really good at that."

"Alison?"

"I went to watch her skate tonight. We talked, and we're best friends again."

"That's great."

"I want her to be partners with us," I went on. "I'm sure Ms. Rand will let the three of us work together. Is that okay?"

"Terrific," he said. "We should have thought of that before."

"The good thing about this idea is that we don't have to build a special display," I pointed out. "We just set up a computer."

"Hey, first you guys are science partners, and

now you're GORF OUT friends. The rumors will be flying."

"Hi, Steve," Eric said.

"Hi, Steve," I grumbled.

"But don't worry about it," Steve went on. "I'm not going to be the person who goes to school tomorrow and tells everyone that Eric and Marcie were seen gorfing out together in a public place."

"Steve?" I said.

"Yeah?"

"Stick a sock in it."

"No sense of humor," he mumbled to himself. Then he turned away to read a yellow sticker on the side of the machine. "That's a thought," he said to himself.

"We've got a science project idea," Eric told him. "We're going to do the game I've been working on in computer club."

"All right!" Steve said.

He and Eric high-fived.

"It's a good idea, but you won't beat my future food," Steve said. "That fifty-dollar bill has my name on it."

"What is your future food, anyway?" I asked.

"The secret ingredient will remain a secret until next Friday, but I can tell you the name of the stuff. It's called a Butzer, after me, of course."

"It sounds like something old lady Bawlf would make," I said.

"It's the next great food. There will soon be

Butzer Bars all over the country. You'll be able to say that you knew me when. Hey, I got to go to the sports store before it closes. I'll see you guys around. Keep gorfing."

After he left, I leaned over to read the yellow label. It said:

You can rent GORF OUT from ACME ARCADE RENTALS. Call 555–8968 and have a GORF OUT delivered to your place of business.

When Steven had read that, he'd said, "That's a thought." I wondered what he'd meant by that?

"Hi, honey," Mom called as I opened the door. "What's new?"

"Nothing," I called back.

"That's nice. I'm in the kitchen."

I wasted another five minutes of my life removing my coat and stuff.

"What's that awful smell?" I asked when I walked into the kitchen. I hopped up, sat on the counter, and stared at the strange mixture in the bowl Mom was holding.

"Marcie, that's not an awful smell. And don't sit on the counter. You know I don't like it. I'm making a healthy breakfast food, Mom's Wonder-Breakfast. Something for *active* people. It's made of granola and dried yogurt and all sorts of fruits."

"Dried yogurt?" I eased down and sat at the table.

"It's healthy and natural. And it's delicious."

"You been talking to Winfred Falkingham?" I asked.

"How is Winny doing? I like that boy."

"He was in the sewer, but I talked him out of it."

"Pardon?"

"Mom, can we talk girl-to-girl for a moment?" I asked.

She made a wide smile. "Of course. I told you that I'm always here." Mom brought the bowl and sat with me at the table. "What's on your mind? "

"Is it a compliment if a boy calls you a fox?"

"Who did that?"

I told her about Eric and the teenager at TacoTime.

"Well, I think Eric was saying something nice," Mom said when I finished.

"But we were talking in social studies about how stuff like that is sexist," I said. "It's really putting down another person. It limits your view of the whole person."

"They teach you that in school?" Mom was surprised. "I don't know what to say, Marcie. I guess it does, in a way. I suppose it's how you use the word, though."

84

"Is it any different from when you called that actor in the James Bond movie a *hunk*?"

"Not really, is it?"

She placed the bowl on the table and leaned back in her chair. "I don't know what to tell you. Things were simpler twenty years ago. I think if a boy had said something like that about me, I'd have felt good. And perhaps that was wrong. Perhaps I should have been upset. How did you feel when you heard it?"

"Good," I told her. "Sort of. But I thought about social studies class."

"The world is definitely changing," Mom said. "In a way, I'm glad I don't have to grow up today."

"That makes me feel good," I told her.

"Oh, I'm not worried about you, dear. If you're asking questions like this now, you're going to do just fine."

And that *really* made me feel good, sort of proud and grown-up. "Thanks, Mom."

"Is there anything else?"

I shook my head. "No . . . I mean, yes. Is Dad okay?"

"Is he okay? What do you mean by that?"

"Is he sick or something?"

"Not as far as I know. Why?" She began to look worried. "Did he tell you he was sick?"

"No. I was just wondering, that's all."

"Why would you start wondering?"

Should I tell her about the REGET? There had to be a good reason for Dad to hide it. And there had to be a good reason for Mom to be acting this way.

"I don't know why I asked," I said. "But I'm allowed strange thoughts once in a while in seventh grade, aren't I? I'm due for hormones."

Mom reached over to feel my forehead to see if I was sick. "Most odd," she said.

Right, I thought. Most odd. She was lying as well. She was covering something up.

I was still awake when Mom and Dad went to bed. I heard Dad in the bathroom. He always gargles with Scope after he brushes his teeth and it's an awful noise, something like a wounded Tyrannosaurus rex must have sounded.

After he'd finished scaring away all the small animals within hearing range, I heard him shuffling around in the cupboard. He was getting the REGET.

Like at breakfast, I knew it wasn't *proper* to spy, but I was so curious. This whole REGET secret was worrying me. I'm part of this family I said to myself. I have a right to know what's going on.

I peeked out my door and across the hall. The bathroom door was half open, and I could see Dad reflected in the mirror. He was dressed in his robe and he had the bottle of REGET in his right hand. He studied his reflection for a few moments, and then he started spraying the stuff over his head.

For the treatment of severe mental disorders, the book had said. I was suddenly struck with a weird thought. Was my father spraying REGET over his head to stop him from going crazy?

I don't know where I got such a stupid thought. It just popped into my head from someplace out in left field. Stupid or not, it surprised me so much that I gasped.

Dad twisted around and peered out the bathroom door. He saw me peeking at him across the hall. "Marcie?" he said. "What are you doing?"

"Nothing," I said.

He opened the door all the way, placed the REGET on the counter, and walked over to me. "You were spying on me, weren't you?"

"I was watching you," I said. "But that doesn't mean I was spying. I was just curious."

"About what?" Now he was talking to me in his principal voice. "Explain yourself immediately."

I was all mixed up. I didn't know what to say. How could I tell him that I knew about the REGET and that he had MPB, and that I knew he'd lied about Dr. Gagesch? And that REGET was used to treat *severe mental disorders*, and that Mom knew he was *losing it*? How could I tell him I knew about something that he wanted to keep a secret from Sarah and me? And that part of me didn't want to hear the answer? What if it *was* something really serious?

"Well, I'm waiting," he threatened. "This had better be good, Marcie."

"I . . . er . . . Dad . . . are you going crazy?" I asked. I knew that was a dumb thing to say, but I really was still mixed up.

"Pardon? Am I what?"

Mom came into the hallway. "What's going on out here?" she asked.

"Marcie wants to know if I'm going crazy." Dad said.

"Pardon?"

"She just asked me if I was going crazy," Dad repeated.

Mom looked at me. "Marcie, why would you ask that?"

Sarah wandered out of her room. "You woke me up," she complained. "Are you really going crazy, Daddy?"

"Apparently I am," Dad said.

"No, you're not," Mom added quickly.

"Thank you, Sharon," he said.

"I didn't mean to say that," I tried to explain. "It's just . . . well . . . why else would you be spraying that stuff over your head if you weren't suffering from a mental disorder?"

"Stuff?" Mom wondered.

"The REGET?" Dad asked me. "You saw me spraying REGET on my scalp?"

"Just because your father is spraying his head doesn't mean that he has a mental disorder," Mom defended him.

"Dad sprays stuff on his head so that he won't go crazy?" Sarah asked.

"Let's get some warm milk and talk about this," Mom suggested.

Ten minutes later we were sitting at the kitchen table drinking warm milk and eating chocolate chip cookies.

I'd told them how I'd found the REGET and looked it up in the medical book. When I finished explaining why I'd asked such a strange question, Mom and Dad both laughed.

"I suppose I was sort of hiding it," Dad said. "It's a little embarrassing to be spraying stuff on my bald head in the hope that it'll grow hair."

"Grow hair? But the medical book said REGET was used to treat mental disorders," I said.

"Not REGET," Dad told us. "But the drug in REGET in another form is used that way. You see, they use this drug in pill form to tranquilize people who are suffering from serious emotional problems. Well, doctors noticed that some men who were taking this pill were growing their hair back. So they took a little of the same drug and mixed it up in a liquid so bald men can spray it on their scalp. That's REGET. I'm using it to try to grow some hair."

"It says it's for MPB. What's that?" I asked.

"That's short for Male Pattern Baldness . . . a fancy way of saying *going bald*," Dad said.

"The package says that it only works on one in five people," Mom said. "I think it's a waste of money."

"And I didn't lie about Dr. Gagesch," Dad concluded. "I didn't want to go to her office for something, so . . ."

"Vain," Mom said.

"Perhaps." Dad nodded. "So I asked her to phone the prescription to the drug store."

"I guess I've been silly," I confessed.

"Your dad and I don't have any secrets from you two," Mom told us.

"I'm just glad nobody is going crazy," Sarah said.

11.
Just Like
the Queen

We had some excellent chuckles about RE-GET over the next few days. When I first told Alison about it at school, she laughed so hard that she had a small accident and needed to change into her gym shorts.

And for the next week, things seemed to click. . . .

Dad dropped my grounding for the weekend. He told me that he agreed with me: I was being punished twice for the same thing, and that the DTs at school were enough.

So I got to go watch Alison skate. She was even more beautiful than at the rehearsal.

Mrs. Bawlf actually made three decent meals: spaghetti, hot dogs, and pizza. Even the Kidney Pot Pies on Thursday weren't all that bad.

The weather warmed up to the low sixties, most weird for November. Ms. Rand said the freak warmth was probably due to the greenhouse effect, and that we should be concerned that we were messing with the atmosphere by burning fossil fuels. I am concerned about pollution and rain forests and ozone and all that, but I'm having a little problem understanding how a warmer winter can be all that bad.

Ms. Rand also said there would be no problem with Alison, Eric, and me working together. She said we could use and move a school computer for the science fair.

Eric's game was really cute. He'd named it THE CHASE. Alison suggested that it was a boring name, and wondered why he didn't call it MUMMY MAZE. Eric thought that was terrific.

MUMMY MAZE is about a little kid with a teddy bear trying to escape from an Egyptian tomb. There are all sorts of mummies and jackals to chase him and steal his teddy bear. Without the bear, he can't get out.

There are mysterious boxes that pop up all over the place. In some of them are snakes and spiders; in others there are jewels or treasure, or the teddy bear, if you lose it.

Mrs. Dawson, the computer teacher, told us, "Considering you used a 128K Apple and a BASIC program, it's an incredible accomplishment."

Eric explained to me how he'd set up a maze for the kid to work through, and how there was only one way to go from point to point, which meant one way to get out of the tomb. I tried to write up the report so that it would make sense to somebody who knew next to nothing about computers, like my father.

"You should be really proud of yourself," I told Eric. "Nobody else in the class could do this."

"Now if I can only pass a math test," he said.

Alison drew the cover for my written work. She also made a large illustrated poster of a scary-looking mummy to place behind the computer on display day.

And, it seemed that all of a sudden, it was next Friday morning and time for the Fifth Street School Science Fair.

Mr. Musgrove, the janitor, moved tables into the gym during morning exercises. Then Ms. Rand assigned us a space at one of the tables for our science projects. A half hour later, the seventh-grade students were set up and ready to be judged.

I checked out the projects of my classmates. Most of them looked great. The gym was full of colored boxes, super models, well-drawn pictures, and neat charts. Everything scientific, from "How Leaves Make Sugar" to "How a Nuclear Power Plant Works," was covered. My dad was going to be pleased.

I made a special note of Tony Alfredo's. I'd

hoped that he'd abandoned his idea of blowing something up. That seemed to be the case. The only thing he'd assembled was a pile of dirt on a piece of plywood. It didn't look much like a bomb.

I was also curious about Steve's effort. He had a plate of brown things on his table. They looked like hockey pucks. A poster behind them said BUTZERS — FOOD OF THE FUTURE. At one point I noticed Mrs. Bawlf wandering around the gym. She stopped to study the Butzers and began talking to Steve.

She obviously liked what she heard because she nodded her head and smiled. She even poked the brown things a few times. I wondered if we'd be having Butzers on our lunch menu soon.

Ms. Rand was wandering about, looking at our efforts. When she got to us, she studied my booklet for a few moments. Eric played the game to show her how it worked.

"Well done," she said. "I'm so pleased you were able to use your individual talents to create such an informative and enlightening display."

That meant she liked it.

"Thanks," Eric, Alison, and I said together.

Eric and Alison moved off in opposite directions to look at the other projects. A short time later, Tony came over to see ours. He tried to play MUMMY MAZE, but kept on losing the teddy bear. "I like video games," he said. "I like them a lot. Your project is great."

"Thanks," I said. "Yours looks sort of interesting, too."

As interesting as a pile of dirt can look, I thought.

"It's okay," he said. "You want to hear something really weird, Marcie?"

"Always."

"Well, I just went to the washroom." Then his eyes went out of focus, and he started nodding his head as if he were thinking about something.

"What's weird about that?" I asked cautiously.

"Guess what I saw in there?"

I wasn't going to say anything. I knew better than that. He was probably setting me up for some gross joke.

When I didn't guess, he told me. "I saw a GORF OUT machine. That's a video game, too."

"I know," I said.

"It's weird, huh? And even weirder, there's some work guys moving other GORF OUT machines into the seventh-grade homerooms. I mean, I didn't think your old man would allow arcade games at school."

"I've got a good idea that my father doesn't know," I said.

Tony scratched his head. "But the work guys who were moving them told me someone from the school had phoned for them. If it wasn't your dad, then who was it?"

"Someone else," I said.

And I know who, I thought.

"All right, everyone," Ms. Rand called. "Take a place next to your projects. We're about to start the judging."

I saw my dad and Mrs. Bompas standing by the gym doors. Mrs. Bompas has been the head of the school board for as long as I can remember. She's a bit on the chubby size. Well, maybe more than a bit.

Mom says that she came to White Falls from someplace in England when she was young. She still has her accent. In fact, when she speaks, I think she sounds like Queen Elizabeth. Alison thinks she's faking it to try to impress people.

Dad went to the microphone on the stage. "Hello, boys and girls," he said. "How are we today?"

"Murmurkle."

"That's great." He smiled. "Before we start the judging, I just want to say how delighted I am with your efforts. Even if you don't win the prize, you are by no means a loser. Each one of you has created a wonderful display, and you should all be extremely proud of yourselves."

We clapped for that because it was true.

"Ms. Rand has already told me how pleased she is," Dad went on.

We applauded that, too.

"And now I'd like to introduce my co-judge, a woman who works hard for all the students and teachers and" — he made a polite chuckle — "the principals in White Falls, the head trustee of our school board, Mrs. Bompas."

We clapped again.

Mrs. Bompas stepped to the microphone and cleared her throat. "I hereby declare the First Annual Fifth Street School Science Fair officially open."

Just like the Queen of England, I thought.

Clap, clap, yet again.

"This looks lovely. Lovely, lovely, lovely," Mrs. Bompas told us.

My father's face must have been hurting. His smile was so wide, it looked as if his cheeks were stapled to his earlobes. His bald head was covered with a thin film of sweat.

"Let's start," Dad said into the mike. "Mrs. Bompas and I will come around to judge your displays."

"Judge mine first," Jennifer called.

My father laughed. "Well, it sounds like Jennifer is excited. And we have to start somewhere. . . ."

Jennifer was decked out in a frilly dress. And she'd done her hair in tight curls.

Everyone was quiet so we could hear what was going on.

"You look lovely today, young lady." Mrs. Bompas said.

"Yes, I do, don't I?" Jennifer made a goofy I'm-so-pretty-and-cute smile. "You should always make an effort to look nice."

I wanted to say, "They're judging a science project, not the Ms. Teeny-Wonderful contest." The principal's daughter thing kept me quiet.

"What a lovely thought," Mrs. Bompas said. "What a lovely, lovely thought. Just think how lovely the world would be if we all made an effort to look nice."

"Barf me out," I heard Steve mumble.

Ms. Rand looked in Steve's direction. He switched to an angelic, innocent look. How come teachers can't see through that?

"And what is your science project about, young lady?" Mrs. Bompas asked.

Jennifer made her stupid smile again. Then she pointed at the fish tank she'd set up on the table. A piece of plastic covered the top. There weren't any fish in the tank. There wasn't even any water. The aquarium was full of mosquitoes.

"Inside this tank are five thousand female mosquitoes," Jennifer began proudly. "Five thousand hungry mosquitoes that want blood."

"All right. This is pretty decent," Eric whis-

98

pered to me. "I didn't know Jennifer could talk that way."

"Did you know that only female mosquitoes bite?" Jennifer asked. "Male mosquitoes eat nectar from flowers. In some species of mosquitoes, the males are born without mouths or stomachs."

"Really?" Mrs. Bompas said. "That *is* very interesting."

"The male mosquito only lives for a few hours, or days, at the most. His only function in life is to . . . to mate." She almost whispered the last word, and her face went a pinky shade. Mrs. Bompas blushed as well. Like I'd told Winny, Mrs. Bompas was a grown-up Jennifer.

"But the female mosquito has a different role," Jennifer went on. "Her job is to lay the eggs for next summer's population. And to form the eggs inside her body, she needs certain proteins. Proteins found in blood. She is the vampire of the insect world."

"You certainly know your facts, young lady," Mrs. Bompas said.

"Of course I do," she said. "Now when a female mosquito inserts her proboscus — that's a fancy word for a mosquito's nose — under your skin, it releases saliva. That's a fancy word for spit." She whispered *spit* as well. "This saliva makes your blood flow smoothly."

"Ewww," Mrs. Bompas said.

"It is so *ewwee*, isn't it?" Jennifer agreed. "That's why my project is so important. It'll stop those *ewwee* things from happening to us."

Ewwee things? I thought.

"The mosquito's need for blood can turn a family picnic into a nightmare," Jennifer went on. "Who hasn't gone to visit a picturesque recreational spot in our great state and not had the day ruined by pesky mosquitoes?"

"None of us," my dad said.

"But help is here." Jennifer held up a spray bottle. It was like the one that my mom uses to spray our house plants.

"Inside this bottle is my magic liquid," Jennifer said. "I mixed it myself. I call it *Bugaway*."

And, then, for the first time in over a week, the feeling washed over me. Something is going to go wrong, I thought.

12.
Bugaway, Boo, and Bloomp

"And what does this Bugaway do, Jennifer?" Dad asked.

Jennifer pointed at the plastic cover. "You see that flap? What do you think would happen if you were to lift it up and place your arm inside the tank?"

She didn't wait for an answer. "I'll tell you what would happen. Your arm would be attacked by five thousand hungry, female mosquitoes. That would be horrible."

"Awful, indeed," my father agreed. He looked a little worried. Maybe he had the feeling, too.

"But after I spray Bugaway on your arm, those same five thousand mosquitoes won't even land. They're afraid of Bugaway. I'd like you to have the honor of being the first person to use it, Mrs. Bompas."

"Well . . ." she said.

I could tell that Mrs. Bompas didn't want to. She was looking at my dad to see if it was okay.

"Oh, it's perfectly safe," Jennifer said. "May I have your arm, please?"

Mrs. Bompas raised her arm slowly and reluctantly.

"Would you pull up your sweater, please?" Jennifer asked.

"Is this all right?" Mrs. Bompas asked my father.

"Of course, it is," Jennifer answered for him. She began to spray Mrs. Bompas's arm.

"Have you tested it?" my dad wanted to know.

Jennifer shook her head. "Not really, but I know it'll work. Would I do something that wasn't terrific?"

"You *are* one of our best students," Dad agreed. "But, still, maybe we should . . ."

She didn't let him finish. "It'll be fine," she said. "You know there's a saying, *leave the best until last.* I think that's silly. I think we should always have the best first. That what being first means. It means you're the best. When you've finished judging the other projects, you'll see what I mean. The first is the best."

Then she tugged Mrs. Bompas closer to the fish tank. "When I lift the cover, you put your arm inside, okay?"

"All right, dear," Mrs. Bompas said quietly. "If you're quite sure."

"You're going to be amazed how Bugaway

works," Jennifer said. Then she quickly lifted the flap on the plastic and helped Mrs. Bompas push her arm into the home of five thousand mosquitoes.

Five thousand bloodthirsty, hungry mosquitoes.

If those bugs were supposed to be afraid of Bugaway, nobody had told them. In less than a second, Mrs. Bompas's arm was covered with a living mass of female mosquitoes.

I'm not sure which opened wider, Mrs. Bompas's eyes, or her mouth. Her whole face seemed to get two sizes bigger.

"OOOOOOOWWWWWWW!" she screamed.

Mrs. Bompas yanked her arm from the tank and swatted the bugs with her other hand. A few hundred mosquitoes scrambled for safety and joined the seventh-grade students in the Fifth Street School gym.

"Oh, my," my father said. "Mrs. Bompas, are you . . . Jennifer, how could you? . . . oh, my."

If Jennifer had just run full speed into a brick wall, she couldn't have looked more stunned. Her chin dropped. "But, but . . ." she mumbled.

That knowing feeling tightened its hold on me. It's started, I thought.

"This is most unpleasant," Mrs. Bompas said as she scratched at the white and red lumps that dotted her arm.

"I'm so sorry," my father apologized. He waved at a bug buzzing around his ear. "Let's leave and have someone look at your arm."

Mrs. Bompas took a deep breath. "No, no," she said in her best Queen voice. "The show must go on, as they say. The other children are waiting. I'll be fine."

Jennifer couldn't believe what had happened. "I must have mixed something wrong. It was supposed to work. I've never done anything like this before."

"I want to see you in my office later," my dad told her.

"Me?" Her state of shock deepened. "Me? In the principal's office? Does this mean I don't get an A plus?"

My father glared at her. "We'll talk later."

"I think I'm going to faint," Jennifer said.

She didn't.

Dad led Mrs. Bompas toward Winfred. "I'm sure Winfred's project will be educational and entertaining," he said. "Winfred has a very scientific mind."

Winfred broke into his dippy grin. "Why, thank you, Mr. Wilder." Then he extended his hand to Mrs. Bompas. "I'm so pleased to personally meet someone with such an important position in our community."

Mrs. Bompas shook Winfred's hand and then returned to scratching her red spots. "What a lovely young man. You are so polite."

"I think it's very important to be polite to each other," Winfred told her.

"What a lovely thought," Mrs. Bompas said. "Imagine how lovely the world would be if we all made an effort to be more polite."

Steve put his finger down his throat and made a gagging sound. Ms. Rand began to look around to see who had made the noise. By the time she checked Steve, he was angelic again. Why didn't she just *know* it was Steve?

Mrs. Bompas studied Winfred's effort.

I grabbed a mosquito flying in front of my face.

My dad pointed to the large poster that Winfred had drawn. It was a picture of a nose. Only it was like the ones you see in a doctor's office, the ones that show the inside of something. "And what have we here?" he asked.

Winfred held up his index finger and touched the tip of his nose. "The nose," he began. "One of our most important organs. It helps us understand our world through the gift of smell. It helps us taste our food. Did you know that if you hold your nose and place a slice of onion on your tongue, you won't be able to tell what it is? For all you know, it could be a piece of apple. The nose is very important."

Mrs. Bompas looked as if she were really interested in what Winfred was saying.

There was a slapping sound somewhere in the

gym as someone squashed a mosquito.

"But the nose is also a pathway to the lungs," Winfred went on. "We use our nose to breathe. We bring outside air into the very inside of our body."

"It's a good illustration," Dad said.

"Thank you, sir. May I tell you about another fascinating function of this important organ?"

"Please do, young man," Mrs. Bompas said.

"Outside air!" Winfred thumped his fist in his hand for effect. "Outside air is full of germs, full of dust, full of things that we don't want inside our bodies. But the nose has its own filter system. Lots of little hairs and boogers. When you pick your nose, Mrs. Bompas, do you ever wonder what a booger really is?"

"What?!" my father said.

"Pardon?" Mrs. Bompas gasped. "When I what?"

"I don't like calling it a booger," Winfred went on. "It's not a polite-sounding word, is it? And I believe that it's important to always be polite. So let's just call it a *boo*. I think that sounds much nicer than booger, don't you?"

"A boo?" Mrs. Bompas covered her mouth. She looked ill.

"A boo traps germs and dust in your nose. It stops the germs from traveling into your lungs. Without a boo or two, you'd get sick."

"What!?" This time, my father shouted. "You

did your science project on . . . on . . ."

"Your nose," Winfred grinned. "And all the wonderful things inside. Would you like to see my drawing of a boo? It's four hundred times life-size."

"No!" my dad yelled.

"I think I'm going to faint." Mrs. Bompas leaned her hand on my dad's shoulder for support.

She didn't.

Winfred was as stunned as Jennifer. "You don't like my project? I thought it was a great idea. I can run home and get my other one. It's on raw sewage treatment, and . . ."

"Enough," my dad said as he guided Mrs. Bompas from the inside of the nose. "I'll see you in my office later as well."

The disaster is beginning to roll, I thought.

"You'll feel much better in a moment," my father told Mrs. Bompas. "Let's take a look at Tony's project. I'm sure Tony will have something that's more . . . er, down-to-earth."

"Right," Tony said. "Mine is not only down-to-earth, it's down *in* the earth." Then he started chuckling like he'd just told a joke.

Mrs. Bompas steadied herself and adjusted her clothing. She took a Kleenex from her purse and wiped her forehead. Then she studied Tony's large pile of dirt on the piece of plywood. My father took a close look at Tony. He seemed worried.

"What is this, young man?" Mrs. Bompas asked.

It took a few seconds for Tony to stop laughing. "It's a volcano. No, it's not a volcano yet. It'll be one when I light it. Then it'll blow up. I figure the best way to get a good mark is to blow something up."

"Light it? Blow something up?" My father scratched a mosquito bite on his neck. "I don't like the sound of that. I can't allow it. We have fire regulations about lighting things in school. And we can't blow anything up."

"It's no big deal, Mr. Wilder," Tony said. "I don't really light nothing. And it's not really a big blow up. I've fixed the inside so it's full of baking soda and a cup of vinegar. I just bump it so that the vinegar spills on the baking soda, and the volcano makes lots of fizz. No problem."

"Well, I suppose that sounds all right," my father said. He didn't seem all that sure about it.

"No sweat." Tony smiled. Then he lifted his arm and thumped the pile of dirt with his fist.

Nothing happened.

"That's weird," Tony said. "That should spill the vinegar. Guess I didn't hit it hard enough."

He raised both arms above his head and smashed them into the dirt.

Tha-dump!

Nothing happened.

Tony stood on his toes, stretched his hands as far as possible, and brought them down with an angry cry. "Aaaarrrggghhh!"

THA-DUMP!!!

There was a soft hissing sound from deep inside the pile of dirt.

"That's better." Tony grinned. "In a second, it'll start coming out the top, and then . . ."

KA-BLLLLLOOOOOMMMMMPPPPP!!!!

13.
Butzers

Tony's pile of dirt vanished in a cloud of pea-sized lumps. Any close-by mosquitoes met their doom. Close-by people got covered in fizzy, pea-sized lumps of dirt, baking soda, and vinegar.

"Well, I never!" Mrs. Bompas cried. She wiped the glop from her face with her Kleenex. "I thought I'd have a lovely time, and now look at me. My outfit is ruined."

My dad used the sleeve of his jacket to remove the muck from his face. "I'm so sorry, Mrs. Bompas. I had no idea. Please send me the cleaning bill."

Tony pulled the glop from his hair. "It wasn't supposed to do that."

"Are you all right?" my father asked Mrs. Bompas.

"Of course I'm not! I've never been . . ."

I didn't hear the rest. I had to turn around to hide my grin. I didn't want Dad to see me. In fact, I thought I was going to laugh.

Even though the science fair had turned into a worse disaster than I could have imagined, it was a *funny* disaster. Even though my dad must have been terribly embarrassed, he looked so *funny* wiping glop from his face and suit.

The rest of the seventh graders didn't share my feelings. They looked shocked, even scared, as if they were going to be punished for the bugs, boos, and bloomps. Everyone except for Alison, who was trying to stifle her own laughter, and Steve, who was chuckling out loud. Ms. Rand's daggered stare stopped him.

When I turned around again, my Dad and Mrs. Bompas were standing next to Eric.

"Are you sure you don't want to clean up before we go on?" my father asked.

Mrs. Bompas brushed the baking soda/dirt from her blouse, and then scratched at the bites on her arm. "Mr. Wilder," she said through her gritted teeth. "Right now, the only thing I wish to do is to finish judging the projects. Then I want to get as far away from Fifth Street School as I can."

"Yes, Mrs. Bompas." He appeared to shrink under her words. "I understand. I'm sorry everything has gone wrong."

"Well, I'm sure that the worst is over with." Her voice dripped with anger. "Who is next?"

"I guess we are," Eric said. "Can I show you our computer game? It's called MUMMY MAZE, and it's . . ."

As Eric explained the game to Mrs. Bompas, my father directed a steely stare at Alison and me. I was trying so hard not to laugh. My father had lumps of fizzing dirt splattered on his shiny head. It looked like he'd been attacked by a flock of sea gulls. Just the thought of that made me smile.

I tried to pretend that I was grinning because I was happy about our science project. I picked up the booklet I'd written, and helped Eric describe the game to Mrs. Bompas.

"Very, very clever," Mrs. Bompas said when I was finished. "And the illustration of the mummy on the poster is so well done."

Alison made sure she took credit for that.

Mrs. Bompas tried playing MUMMY MAZE, but lost her teddy bear right away. She was worse than useless. Then again, a lot of adults are. It's almost as if they think computers are going to bite them.

But she seemed to have a good time. By the time they moved on, both she and my dad were smiling.

"Now that was more like it," Mrs. Bompas said.

"Everything will be fine now," my father assured her. "Nothing will go wrong."

And I suppose that, except for one, the rest of the projects would have been as harmless as ours. They would have impressed the judges with how much the Fifth Street School seventh graders knew about plants, animals, chemistry, physics, and all sorts of other scientific wonders. Mrs. Bompas would have had a *lovely* time. Unfortunately, there was one project waiting, hidden in the rest, which would complete the science fair disaster.

Mrs. Bompas and my father headed toward Steve Butz and the Food of the Future.

"Howdy," Steve said. "You have now arrived at the project that is going to win fifty big ones."

My dad eyed the brown hockey pucks on Steve's plate. Then he read the poster.

"Future Food?" he said. "This isn't going to bite or explode, is it? It doesn't have anything to do with the inside of your nose, does it?"

"Of course not," Steve told him. "My project can only amaze you. I call these little burger-shaped things Butzers. That's after my last name, Butz. Get it?"

"That's a lovely idea," Mrs. Bompas said. "It's so creative."

"Thanks," Steve said. "But I'm not attached to the name or anything. I'll change it if you think it'll help me win first prize. I don't mind calling them Wilders or Bompasers."

"Are you trying to bribe the judges?" Mrs. Bompas said with a smile.

"Would it help?" Steve asked.

"Steve!" my father warned.

"I was just joking," Steve said quickly.

"You have such a delightful personality, young man," Mrs. Bompas told him.

Alison and I looked at each other with wrinkled noses.

"Anyway," Steve went on. "A Butzer is a new food for the future. As the population of our planet increases, we'll start to run out of food. Our diet will have to change. Do you know that it takes eight pounds of grain to grow one pound of beef?"

"Really?" Mrs. Bompas said.

"In the future, there will be so many people that we won't be able to waste that much grain to feed a cow. We'll have to eat it ourselves."

"That really makes one think, doesn't it?" my father said.

"And we'll have to search for new stuff to eat," Steve continued. "That's where a Butzer comes in. It will fill that food gap."

"Well, you're certainly thinking about the welfare of us all, aren't you?" Mrs. Bompas said.

"Sure." Steve nodded. "Anything to get fifty bucks."

"What is in a Butzer?" Mrs. Bompas wondered.

"Ah!" Steve grinned. "I got the idea for a Butzer when my dad said he was going ice fishing in Canada. It just clicked into place. Fishing, I thought — there's the perfect idea. Fishing and future food."

"Fish," Mrs. Bompas nodded. "What a lovely

idea. I enjoy fish very much. It's a very health-ful thing to eat." She reached over, broke a hockey puck in half, and began to eat the future food.

"Hmmm," she smiled. "This is lovely. It doesn't really taste like fish, but it tastes lovely."

"It isn't fish," Steve said. Then he held out the plate to my father. "Would you like to try some, Mr. Wilder."

My dad reached for one of the brown disks and took a cautious nibble. "They are quite tasty," he agreed.

Mrs. Bompas finished the first half and reached for the half left on the plate. "If it isn't fish, what is it, then?" she asked with a full mouth.

"It's even healthier than fish," Steve said. "In fact, some fish eat it."

"Oh, yes." My father nodded. "I think I know. I was reading about this in *National Geographic*. This is algae, isn't it? This is that blue-green algae that's supposed to be so good for you."

"Algae?" Mrs. Bompas asked as she took an-other bite.

"Microscopic plants," my dad explained. "The simplest form of plant life. Full of the basic build-ing blocks of life. A lot of fish eat it."

"Isn't that the scummy stuff that grows on the side of fish tanks?" Alison whispered.

"I wonder where Steve got algae from?" Eric said.

"I have a feeling that it's something else," I told them.

"It's not algae," Steve said. "I wouldn't feed you plants. I got this at the sport store. In the bait section. Butzers are worms. Night crawlers, to be exact."

"Worms?!" Mrs. Bompas gasped. You could see her throat tighten up.

"Night crawlers?" my father wheezed.

"Butzers are easy to make," Steve told them. "All you have to do is dry up the worm. Then you mash it until it's like powder. Add a little salt and a little oatmeal to hold it together, and you get a Butzer, the Future Food. Neat, huh?"

"AAAAARRRRUUUUCCCCKKKK!!!!" Mrs. Bompas screamed and spit out the mouthful of Butzer.

Without being too gross, let's just say my father had another lump of stuff on his bald head.

After disposing of Steve's future food, Mrs. Bompas ran out of the gym, sort of screaming . . . half yelling and half crying. It was an interesting sound. One I'll remember for a long time.

My father wore anger and embarrassment with a red face. He stomped down the hall to the office. We heard his door slam from the gym.

I walked over to a grinning Steve Butz. He offered me a Butzer. "Want one?"

"You did that on purpose, didn't you? All that talk about winning the prize was bull, wasn't it?

You knew Mrs. Bompas was going to go snake when she found out she was eating worms."

"Marcie," he said. "Do I look like somebody who would do something like that?"

"Is the sky blue?" I answered.

That finished the science fair. Nobody else was judged. Ms. Rand ushered us back to class. She acted embarrassed, too, as if it were her fault that things had gone wrong.

Everybody was excited to find GORF OUT machines in our homerooms and the washrooms. They didn't stay long, though. My dad had them picked up within an hour.

14.
Worth a Try

Bugging Time that night started in the usual way. Sarah complained that we never pay any attention to what she says during Bugging Time.

"That's nonsense, Suds," Mom said. "Of course, we do. It's just that your father has more important things to say tonight."

That was Mom's way of turning Bugging Time over to him so he could get rid of his frustrations caused by the science fair.

"I have never been so embarrassed . . ." he began.

I sort of tuned out a little. I knew what he was going to say, so I just listened for the key words.

". . . Such a great idea . . . who would have thought? . . . nothing could go wrong . . . what got into that boy's head? . . . a booger!? . . . thousands of mosquitoes buzzing around the school . . . what got into that girl's head? . . . the inside of your nose?! . . . dried worms?! . . . future food?!

. . . what got into that boy's head?! . . . I actually ate night crawlers . . . exploding volcanoes?! . . . what got into that boy's head? . . . fizzy, messy glop everywhere . . . Mrs. Bompas was so brave, but eating worms . . . how can I show my face at the board meeting? . . . GORF OUT machines in the washrooms . . ." and so on.

We went through the main course and dessert listening to Dad.

"They were just accidents, Grigg," Mom said after he was finished. "You couldn't have known what was going to happen."

"But you should have listened to me," I said. "I had a feeling, remember? Next time, maybe you should believe me."

"Nobody ever listens to *me*," Sarah moaned.

My dad sighed. "All right, Marcie. Next time you feel something will end up in a mess, I'll definitely take you more seriously."

"Great," I said. "I have a feeling it's going to be a real mess to decide who should win first prize for their project. Well, since the project Alison, Eric, and I did was the only one you and Mrs. Bompas looked at that didn't blow up or fly away or stuff, maybe you should give us the prize."

Dad shook his head. "Ms. Rand and I decided nobody would win. That's the only fair way. And that will avoid all potential problems."

It was worth a try.

"Okay, I have a feeling about Mrs. Bawlf's

lunches. You see, I think she's really feeding the students at Fifth Street School secret chemicals in an attempt to turn us into a race of flesh-eating mutants."

"Be serious," Mom said.

"I am."

"I told you I'm watching the menu," my dad said. "If I see a need, I'll speak to Mrs. Bawlf."

"Speaking of a mess," I went on. "You know that ski trip Mom has planned for spring break?"

"That is not a subject I wish to discuss," she said. "That subject is not allowed during Bugging Time. That may not seem fair, but making sure you're more active is more important than fairness."

"Oh, but I just want to tell you that I'd love to go. If . . ."

"If what?" Mom asked.

"If you let me go to Florida with Alison at Christmas when she visits her dad. I promise I won't complain about freezing my butt on the side of a mountain if you let me do that."

"Has she invited you?" Dad asked.

I nodded. "Wouldn't that be great?"

"I want to go, too," Sarah said.

"You can't because you're not invited," I told her.

She started to pout.

"You'd want to leave us for Christmas?" Mom

said. "You know how nice it is to have a family Christmas."

"I've had twelve of them," I reasoned. "What's it going to hurt if I miss one? And I promise that come spring break, I'll pretend skiing is my favorite sport."

"Well, I . . ." Mom began. "What do you think, Grigg?"

"I think we should think about it," Dad said.

"So you're not saying no?" I asked.

"Your mother and I will discuss it."

"All right!"

"I want to go, too," Sarah repeated.

"Before we go on," Dad said, "there's one thing I have to tell you, one important thing that got pushed aside during today's excitement. It's something you have to think about, Marcie."

"What's that?" I said.

"Do you remember Ms. Fletcher, the principal of Seventh Avenue Junior High? She came over for the barbecue last summer?"

"Sort of."

"Well, I was speaking to her at a meeting last week, and I was telling her about your problem. You know, how you felt about being at Fifth Street School, how tough it was to have your father as principal. Well, Ms. Fletcher said she'd be delighted to have you transfer to her school. Why don't you think about it for a while? We could arrange it for after Christmas vacation. I know that's a month away, but it's the most logical time."

"I don't have to do much thinking about that," I said. "Even if it *is* tough being the principal's daughter, I think I'd rather stay at Fifth Street School."

"How come?" Sarah asked.

"I'd hate to miss Dad's great ideas," I said. "What would I do without another disaster to look forward to?"

About the Author

Martyn Godfrey is one of Canada's most popular writers of books for young people. He has published over thirty books, including the *Carol and Wally* series, *Can You Teach Me to Pick My Nose?* and, with Scholastic, *I Spent My Summer Vacation Kidnapped Into Space*. He lives in St. Albert, Alberta, with his two teenage children, Marcus and Selby.

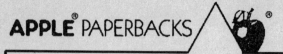